His thumb traced perilously close to the corner of her mouth, and Ryan leaned in. Stella hadn't forgotten this, that was for sure. Breath brushing across lips. Calloused fingers drawing a lazy pattern—

"Wait, what are we doing?" She sprang back, whacking her head on the hatch in the process. "Ouch." She rubbed the aching spot.

"Not thinking, that's for sure." He rubbed his jaw. "Kinda wish you'd come to your senses about ten seconds later, though."

She grabbed his jacket from where it was draped over the back seat and shoved it at him, then put her hands on her hips. "You forgot about me easily enough when you turned me away from that ranch."

His eyes shuttered closed. "Crap, Stella, I'm so sorry..."

"You should be." In more ways than he knew. "Doesn't mean you were wrong about the end result, though. I'm not the small-town girl you need."

And if she gave in and kissed him, even for curiosity's sake, she'd be leaving Sutter Creek in more turmoil than when she arrived.

Dear Reader,

Have you ever caught yourself wondering how different things would be if you altered just one formative past decision? Stella Reid has buried any doubts about her youth under a demanding hedge fund career. She's the opposite of nostalgic about her small-town upbringing and is determined to forget how head over heels she was for Ryan Rafferty. But when her life in Manhattan crumbles, she returns to Sutter Creek to regroup. She's utterly unprepared to face Ryan, who's no longer the heartbreaker bad boy who deserted her after graduation.

Sheriff Ryan Rafferty knows how to regroup better than anyone—moving past his misdemeanor record to get elected small-town sheriff was anything but easy. He'd love Stella to see just how much he's changed. Lucky for him, it's impossible to avoid anyone in Sutter Creek. Between grandparent shenanigans and getting stuck in a cabin in the woods after a snowstorm, love has plenty of chances to work its magic on this stubborn duo.

I'd love to hear your thoughts on *Snowbound with the Sheriff*. You'll find me on Facebook, Instagram and Pinterest (laurelgreerauthor). Or check out the rest of the Sutter Creek series on my website, laurelgreer.com!

Love,

Laurel

Snowbound with the Sheriff

LAUREL GREER

HARLEQUIN
SPECIAL
EDITION

Recycling programs for this product may not exist in your area.

ISBN-13: 978-1-335-40462-6

Snowbound with the Sheriff

Harlequin Enterprises ULC
22 Adelaide St. West, 40th Floor
Toronto, Ontario M5H 4E3, Canada
www.Harlequin.com

Printed in U.S.A.

Raised in a small town on Vancouver Island, **Laurel Greer** grew up skiing and boating by day and reading romances under the covers by flashlight at night. Ever committed to the proper placement of the Canadian *eh*, she loves to write books with snapping sexual tension and second chances. She lives outside Vancouver with her law-talking husband and two daughters. At least half her diet is made up of tea. Find her at www.laurelgreer.com.

Books by Laurel Greer

Harlequin Special Edition

Sutter Creek, Montana

To my readers—thank you for coming to Sutter Creek to find love and hope.

Chapter One

Stella Reid hadn't cried since she was eighteen. And even though a lump the size of her rental car filled her throat, she didn't plan on starting now. She squinted through the snow that flecked the windshield, gripping the steering wheel tight enough to make her fingers cramp. Side benefit to her late flight into Bozeman: it was too dark to see if a streak of bright red paint still marked the second pole past the turnoff to Moosehorn Lake.

There weren't any other cars on the road to keep her company, either. A snowstorm on a Thursday night meant the locals went to bed at nine, she supposed. Turning up the volume on the stereo, she glanced at the odometer, then the clock on the dashboard. Why did the small ski town where she'd grown up have to be so far away from civilization? She'd left the place in her dust to go to college, and could count on two fingers the number of times she'd returned since.

Her plans had eclipsed Montana far before the biggest mistake of her life. Being eighteen and sitting on the side of the road, handcuffs biting into her wrists and rain pelting her face, had only solidified her drive to get out and put her mark on the world.

She'd climbed the rungs of a Manhattan hedge-fund firm, but it was a ladder that was currently collapsing, one workplace rumor at a time. At least she'd avoided handcuffs this go-round.

But she was still going to land on her ass in Sutter Creek and watch her life crumble around her.

Her head swirled faster than the flakes falling outside the vehicle. In the face of her firm's fraud scandal, which would go public any day, her high-school shenanigans—wrecking Ryan Rafferty's uncle's car and getting threatened with the loss of her scholarship—sounded like a picnic. And she didn't even know how to begin removing the wedge she'd put between her and her family since she'd blown the whistle on her CIO six months ago.

Six months of distance? Try your whole life.

Sighing, she forced herself to focus on the dimly lit, snowy road. Emotional reunions weren't her thing, and she doubted her half siblings were in the mood to hear her out. But she had to start somewhere, right? Making herself useful with repairs to the family's veterinary clinic expansion seemed to be her best bet. She'd keep busy while she waited to see if her career imploded after this morning's information leak at the firm. God, when was the last time small-town USA had more options for forward movement than New York?

She swore to herself. Shaking her head, she tapped the built-in Bluetooth controls. She told her phone to call her half brother, Lachlan. When she'd contacted him this morning to tell him she was finally hopping on a flight for a visit, he'd mentioned something about a work bee two days from now, on Saturday. Maybe she could get a few more details out of him while she had nothing better to do than drive. Provided he was willing to talk. He hadn't done a very good job lately of hiding how pissed off he was over how little she'd been in contact.

But facing his temper was preferable to letting her mind drift to that telephone pole a mile back, and all the memories she didn't want to revisit during her trip.

Getting knocked up. Getting arrested. Loving—and losing—Ryan Rafferty.

Her brother answered after three rings.

"Stella? You here? I don't see your car outside." He yawned audibly.

"Not yet. I just passed RG Ranch. Or whatever it's called now."

He chuckled. "Still the same."

"Like everything else in town."

"No, I'd say you've missed out on a hell of a lot of new things." His lighthearted tone vanished. "Starting with your niece. She rolled over the other day. And you haven't even gotten to hold her yet."

Stella's heart squeezed. "I know. Like I said, I would have come sooner but—"

"Work got in the way," Lachlan snapped.

She exhaled. There was the anger she'd been expecting. The anger she *deserved*. The problem with being in the middle of a massive securities-fraud investigation was not being able to tell anyone about it. Including her family. Not when her niece had been born, or when, back in November, a fire had ripped through an old barn that Lachlan was in the process of converting into a search-and-rescue dog school. Stella had been stuck in a boardroom in Manhattan with a wire taped under her blouse when she got the news their sister, Maggie, had been admitted to the burn unit. She had so much she had to make up for.

"If I'm going to keep paying the seed money for your business, I need to keep my job," she said. "And there was no way to leave my ongoing work project partway through." She'd only managed to get leave from the investigators yesterday. They'd decided that the rumors swirling around the firm necessitated Stella being somewhere else, so they'd approved her request to go to Sutter Creek, provided she surrender her passport and agree to return when required.

"Maggie and I needed you to be here, not just to

play the wallet. But you've never been one for home, Stell. I don't know why I thought Laura's birth or the fire would be different."

His "I'm not mad, I'm disappointed" tone was worse than his earlier curtness. She was never going to be part of her half siblings' close-knit duo, not with them being full siblings and Stella having a different mom. Maggie and Lachlan had grown up in Chicago and both had moved to Sutter Creek after they'd graduated from the elite prep school Stella would have sold her soul to attend. She'd wanted nothing more than to be in a big city, so had only spent the summers with them during their childhood. And her mom had never gotten over Stella's dad's infidelity. Encouraging a bond between Stella and her "cheating husband's brats" had been crazy low on the family priority list.

Fear struck Stella. Would two weeks of helping with the rebuild even put a dent in all that? Picking up a paintbrush on Saturday seemed too small an effort. But where else could she start? "Count me in for slapping some paint on a wall this weekend."

"We're starting with framing and drywalling," he corrected.

"A hammer, then." Getting to participate in the barn rebuild would be a small beam of hope amid the dimness surrounding her career. "I really do want to help out. Even if I have a few things to catch up on."

"Almost twenty years' worth of *things*, Stella,"

he growled. "You've actively put more distance between you and us."

No, between her and Sutter Creek. She hadn't in-
tentionally widened the sibling divide.

Or had she?

"Well, you've got me for two weeks. All of me."

"And we're not going to turn down an extra set of
hands." He sighed. "You should know that Ryan—"

"I don't want to talk about him." She refused to
waste any valuable brain energy on Ryan Rafferty.
When she'd needed him most, he'd cut off all contact.
Half a lifetime had passed. It was no longer relevant,
no matter how much she'd lost in the aftermath of
their breakup.

Deal with the things you can fix.

"I'm really looking forward to getting to know
Laura and Marisol." She yawned. Oh, man. Her hasty
escape from New York was catching up to her. She
did not have the energy to meet new people tonight.
If she rolled in half-asleep and midargument with
Lachlan, she'd make a terrible first impression. "I
know you offered that I could stay at your place, but
I think it's better that I grab a room at one of the ho-
tels." Predicting she'd need a place to recharge, she'd
booked in at the Sutter Mountain Hotel mid-flight.
This conversation was only confirming she'd made
the right decision.

A long pause filled the SUV. Had she lost the connection? "Lachlan?"

"You're not even going to stay with us?" He

sounded like he couldn't decide whether to be relieved or hurt.

Ouch.

"You have enough going on without having to play host. I'll come have coffee in the morning before you head off to work."

He swore under his breath. The quiet bite in the word reverberated through Stella.

"We could invite Gramps, too," she suggested. Their grandfather had moved home from his winter residence in Arizona to help out Maggie at the veterinary clinic after the fire. Maggie's burns limited what she could do with her animal patients, and their grandfather had stepped back in as the main veterinarian.

"Did you even bother to tell him you were arriving?" Lachlan said, his voice a hairbreadth from a shout.

"Of course. I texted him before I left New York." They'd have plenty of time to catch up in more detail.

"And the bathroom I spent cleaning today? And Marisol forgoing napping when Laura napped so that she could wash the sheets and get the spare room ready for you? You didn't think to text us, too?"

All right, that *was* a full-on shout. She lowered her voice, hoping that if she was calm, he'd follow suit. "I left so quickly, I lost sight of the details. I didn't mean to put you out. How about I come for a drink tonight, then? Meet Marisol, at least. I assume Laura's asleep."

"So's Marisol—she passed out on the couch a half hour ago, waiting for you to get here. So if you don't want to stay here, there's no point in coming by tonight. What's one more day, when it's been, what, over a year since I last saw you?"

Guilt stabbed her clean through and acid burned her throat. "This was really my first opportunity to take holidays. The past few months... Like I've said a hundred times, I've been tied up. I'm sorry."

"Maybe one of these days, I'll actually believe you. See you tomorrow."

He hung up.

Her stomach lurched, and she clutched the wheel. Okay. She was going to need her quiet night in the hotel to strategize on how to begin to make amends with Lachlan.

If only I could be honest.

She winced. *Taking holidays...* Bit of a stretch. More accurately, she'd been forced to take a leave of absence. The authorities investigating her firm's CIO had told her to stay away from the office until the investigation was complete and charges were laid. Focusing on anything other than work had been impossible since the moment when, newly promoted and with access to more information than she'd ever had as an analyst, she realized some of the practices of the senior members of the firm were shifty as hell. She'd been a key part of the case, right up until her role as whistleblower was leaked internally a couple of days ago. All problems she wasn't able to explain to her siblings because of the non-disclosure agreement she'd signed.

Her marching orders for the next two weeks were clear—visit her family, but no breaking her silence. Either the investigators would finish gathering evidence and charge her colleagues, exonerating Stella, or the whole mess would go public, make the national news and people would naturally assume she had snitched to cover her own ass. Either way, losing her anonymity meant her name was mud at the firm.

Be a whistleblower, the district attorney said. *It'll be kept confidential*, the SEC authorities said. *They can't fire you—we promise.* Or her favorite: *your coworkers will thank you.*

Wrong, wrong, wrong.

Well, *right*. Ethically, she'd made the right choice.

And she couldn't control whether, or how fast, charges were laid against the fraudsters, or if her attempt to be the good guy would mean losing everything. But she could use these two weeks to rebuild some damage she *had* caused. Her half siblings deserved better than the arm's length she'd held them to over the years.

Stella contemplated calling Maggie to check in, but her reserves were drained to zero. She narrowed her gaze on the two dark ruts of asphalt, ribbons of black running through the world of white. Slowing for one of the few stoplights along the two-lane highway, she waited for a pickup to turn, but a gust of wind shook the car, bringing a sheet of snow across her windshield. Her pulse jumped, and she took her foot off the accelerator for a moment.

God, she hated this road. Had it always been this far a drive from Bozeman? Then again, in high school, any time she'd made the trek into town, she'd usually been preoccupied by a certain handsome cowboy in the driver's seat.

As a teen, she'd scrambled for every scholarship dollar, desperate to get to college without hurting her mom by asking her dad for help. And then Ryan had come along, wearing a Stetson and a broody smile, oozing teenage testosterone. She'd lost her head. And almost lost her shot at an upward trajectory.

He might have covered for her when they'd been stupid kids, giving her the chance to earn her place in the upper echelon of New York's financial world. Might have pulled Maggie from the fire, too. But just because he'd saved both Stella's ass and her half sister's life didn't mean she was required to look back on him fondly.

He'd earned her gratitude, but he'd never earn back her loyalty.

She pressed the accelerator just a hint more. The weather was crap, but the SUV had all-wheel drive and winter tires, and the faster she got to the hotel, the better. She needed to sleep. Lick her wounds a little. And show up at Lachlan's in the morning, ready to make amends.

The dark stretch of road made it feel like she was the only person in the universe, except for whoever was in the car stopped at an upcoming intersection. Headlight beams lit the interior of her vehicle as she passed. White, to red and blue—

She startled, and her car swerved a little. The tires pulled in the shallow snow ruts, and her heart rate kicked up again. She steadied the vehicle, taking a deep breath to calm her pulse. Oh, crap. A cop. What the hell? She was going maybe two miles over the speed limit. Maybe she wasn't the guilty one.

The siren blipped.

Ugh, definitely for her. She eased over to the side of the road, tires jittering as they caught the snow. Great. She was going to be even later checking in, if she had to spend any length of time explaining to the officer why they were completely in the wrong for pulling her over. She turned the key in the ignition, cutting off Chris Cornell mid-chorus.

By the time she had the window rolled down and was being blinded by a flashlight, her chest burned with irritation.

Snow swirled in through the open window, stinging her face. She squinted into the bright beam—with no streetlights, all she could see was a silhouetted cowboy hat pulled low over the officer's face and broad, male shoulders.

"Do you want my license and registration?" Stella asked, holding the documents out for the still, silent man. "It's a rental. And I wasn't speeding." *And I just want to go to bed, and this highway is the worst because the last time I was on it, I got arrested—*

"Holy God," the officer said, gripping the open window ledge with a black-gloved hand. He lowered his flashlight. A gold star on his chest glinted in the beam. "Stella."

"Ryan?" Fragments of her past sliced at her. Soulful, guarded eyes. Strong hands. A dry wit that made her laugh so hard she couldn't breathe.

And ending up utterly, painfully alone. Having to deal with losing their baby without him even having known she was pregnant.

She blurted out the first thought that made it to her mouth. "You have a criminal record. How the hell are you the sheriff?"

Chapter Two

Ryan clenched his teeth to stop his jaw from hanging open. If there was ever a time to rely on his impervious-sheriff face, it was now. He'd expected a routine traffic stop of an out-of-towner.

Not Stella Reid.

Not the physical remainder of his only heartbreak, sitting wide-eyed in the driver's seat of a rental car in an expensive-looking wool coat.

He lifted his flashlight.

The beam fell on the set of blue eyes etched permanently on his soul. Catching her squint, he directed the light toward the dashboard. Had she forgotten he'd pled out to a misdemeanor? And was she really surprised by his occupation? He would have thought his name and position would have come up at some point. She must have specifically told her siblings not to mention him. Though his role in saving Maggie from that fire must have been mentioned at least once.

He put on a neutral tone to match his expression. "Been so long you didn't recognize me, Stella?"

The last time he'd laid eyes on her, she'd been trudging off to his grandmother's car, having just been released from handcuffs. Also on the side of the road. Also with lights flashing.

It'd been rain pelting his face then, as opposed to today's snow. And his final words to her—*I'll do this, but after, we're done*—were still imprinted on his soul.

Hers, too, apparently, because he couldn't think of the last time she'd visited. Almost ironic that when he'd pulled Maggie from the barn blaze, he'd given Stella a reason to come home. It was the opposite of when he'd taken all the blame for stealing his uncle's car, and made her promise to leave so she could achieve her dreams.

She lifted her chin, gaze hardening more during each long second. "It's pitch-black out here. And your hat's hiding your face." She waved her fingers in a circle and pointed at his chest. "And, you know, the law-enforcing cop getup."

He flicked up the brim of his hat, exposing more of his skin to the heavy January snow. Once upon a time, he'd seen her in a future that hadn't been for him. She represented a part of him that he wanted to leave long in the past. But those eyes still held sway over him. "Better?"

"Better would be you *not* having pulled me over, and being three minutes closer to my hotel room."

He sent her a questioning look. Hard to believe Lachlan and Maggie wouldn't have offered to put Stella up. Maybe the division between the siblings went deeper than he'd realized. God knew Maggie had taken eighteen years—and a life-saving grab out of an inferno—to forgive him for dumping Stella. Who knew what issues the Reids were still holding on to? But Stella's choice of lodgings was not his concern. Her road speed was.

"You were driving too fast for conditions," he said.

"I was going the speed limit."

"Sure, if you call five over the speed limit. Which is unsafe in the snow. Did your rental company provide you with chains?"

"Yes." Stella pressed her lips together. "I figured I didn't need them until it started sticking to the road more."

Oh, man, the ire spitting from those words. Was she still holding on to resentment from how he'd handled things after they broke up? He'd have thought she'd be more apt to thank him than to still be angry. The night of his arrest, the deputy had threatened her with felony charges, mocked her about losing her scholarship, until Ryan had lied and said he'd stolen his uncle's antique truck for their midnight joyride without her knowing. It had made sense—she, having been the relative angel to his foible-prone teen self. He'd been guilty, after all. No need for both of them to suffer the consequences.

He'd made it clear that, in taking the blame for her, they were done. He'd thought she'd agreed to the plan. But weeks after his plea bargain, she'd come looking for him at the ranch where he was working off his community-service hours. Why, he didn't know—he'd never asked. He'd meant it when he'd ended things, so he'd had a crusty old cowboy turn her away.

A jerk move, sure, though necessary to carry out the new start they'd both needed. Her, away from his bad influence. Him, figuring out how not to be one.

The problem with earning back his good name was that it was impossible to ever feel he'd done enough.

He cleared his throat. "Just make sure you keep the chains in the vehicle in case you're on a road where the snow is deeper."

"You're so official."

"It's my job," he said, clenching the door frame harder.

She shook her head in disbelief. "Eighteen-year-old Ryan wouldn't believe that if he tried."

"No, but I didn't have much vision back then. And I was damn lucky. Otherwise I'd probably be living inside the detention center, not in charge of the people who run it." He intended to continue on the straight and narrow indefinitely, including winning an election this coming fall. Something easier to do if the townsfolk weren't reminded of his past. And reminder number one? Sitting in the driver's seat in front of him.

Hopefully Stella's visit would be a short one.

"If you're that important, surely you had something better to do than lurk in the shadows, waiting for some law-abiding citizen to come along so you could pull them over unfairly," she sniped.

He blinked at her challenge. He used to love it when she got snarky. The snap in her voice that had promised a hell of a good time when they made up. Kissing in the nook behind the high-school music room, in the back of his grandma's Oldsmobile, in the loft of her family's barn… And with those plump, rosy lips? He bet she'd be even better at it now.

Jesus, Rafferty. Reel it in.

Those lips weren't, and wouldn't ever be, his to kiss again. Not if he wanted to keep the star on his coat. He questioned her with a stony look. "Should have known you'd fall into the category of drivers who try to argue their way out of a ticket."

"You're going to give me a *ticket*?"

Damn right, he was. They'd had a fatality on this stretch of road over the Christmas holidays and were cracking down on speeders. Plus, it was better to have her good and mad at him. More likely she'd keep her distance that way. "Ticketing people who are driving dangerously is also my job."

Her cheeks flamed red, illuminated by his flashlight. "More dangerous than driving a stolen vehicle?"

He cocked an eyebrow at her. Yeah, he'd screwed up plenty with this woman. But he was on the clock and wouldn't make exceptions. "I paid my debt. Did you?"

"You…you can't… Statute of limitations—"

"You're fine, Stella. Except for the speeding."

"Take my driver's license." She shoved her paperwork into his hand. "I've never had a ticket—don't I deserve a warning?"

And have people question why he'd let his ex-girlfriend off when she was legitimately speeding? Let *Stella* think he still had a soft spot for her? That wouldn't fly. "Excuse me while I go run this."

A sharp curse followed him back to his patrol truck. He ran her New York license, unsurprised that she'd been telling the truth concerning her driving record. She'd never been a liar.

That label was reserved for him.

He'd contemplated apologizing years ago, but had decided it was better to leave well enough alone. Maybe he'd been wrong on that. No matter—the side of the highway wasn't the place for it.

He wrote up the ticket, gripping the pen as he printed her name in triplicate. *Reid, Stella Beth.* Not

Rafferty, like he'd caught her scribbling in a note-book once. The naivete of youth.

Tipping his hat back down to fend off the snow, he returned to her window.

She'd turned on the overhead light and was read-ing something on her cell. Snowflakes blew in through her window, landing on her black coat. Be-tween her visible anger, her designer clothing and the way she'd scraped her blond hair back into a se-vere bun, she looked untouchable. Out of his league.

Not everything had changed since they were kids.

He handed her the ticket. "I won't pretend I made smart choices that night, Stella. But I've done my best to make up for it."

She stared at him for a long second. "I'm trying to tell myself that what you did for me that night outweighs how you treated me the day I came to the ranch. It definitely should balance out."

"We'd agreed to a clean break."

"Yeah, but I—" Her gaze shifted from his face, and he couldn't help but notice how her hands shook a little as she put her phone in her purse, then folded the paper into a neat square and dropped it into the empty cup holder. "How many people besides you see the tickets you issue?"

"A few," he said.

She swore.

"What?"

"No need to be the town criminal again," she grumbled.

"You never were, Stella. That was me. That's what I agreed to." Shame nipped under his collar, a bite worse than the cold fingers of wind trying to freeze his skin.

"Well, clearly you're doing okay despite all that. Are we done here? I'm sure you have someone or something to get home to."

"Just a dog and an empty bed," he said.

Something approaching satisfaction flickered across her face before she squeezed her eyes shut for a second. "Not my business."

He couldn't stop the corner of his mouth from quirking up at her clipped tone. She wasn't entirely unaffected. And that fragment of vulnerability— he craved it. *Still.* He'd spent countless moments in high school coaxing those beats of emotion out of her. And it was still as much of a victory.

"How long are you staying?"

"Two weeks. Enough time to help Lachlan and Maggie run the work bees."

"I committed to helping them, too. I'll see you there." Not that he was looking forward to it. Wanting anything to do with Stella Reid was asking for trouble. He removed his cowboy hat and ran a hand through his hair before fixing the hat back on. The cold made his scalp tingle, matching the rush of panic skimming down his limbs. "It might have been a long time ago, but it still hurt like hell when we left things so undone."

She let out a disbelieving cough. "*We* left things undone? Try again, Sheriff."

He shook his head slowly. Okay. He *had* been wrong about not calling to apologize. Maybe they could arrange to meet privately. "Given you're in town, we should take the opportunity to talk. Clear the air."

"Since when do you talk?" she scoffed.

Her disbelief rubbed at him and he cringed, like when anyone petted his Labrador backward. Taking a deep breath, he reminded himself she was basing her judgment of his character on who he'd been as a troubled boy, not a man. "It's what adults do."

"Nice high horse there, Ryan. I suppose you're also looking for hero worship for having saved Maggie?"

"No, I—"

But before he could put his words in order, she started her car and drove off.

A good reminder. She was all business. Manhattan and designer coats. And for the sake of being the opposite, it was better that she leave him in her dust.

No one had come close to touching his heart the way Stella Reid had. And if he started to look for similarities between the girl he'd loved and the woman she'd become, he'd risk everything he'd worked so hard to build.

Chapter Three

Stella made it about a hundred yards down the road before Ryan pulled his truck off the shoulder and started to follow her. Great. Just what she needed as she made her way to the hotel—a witness to her *not* staying with one of her siblings. Something else for which he could not so subtly judge her.

Ryan's suggestion that they talk was ill-advised, but it had been his insinuation that she'd acted like a child that had pissed her off. And how weird was it to have him be the one pushing for a conversation? She'd *learned* emotional walls from that man. But it hadn't always been that way. She'd poked at him for years, trying to get him to share as he went through the highs and lows with his father, ending with his dad's overdose. However, he'd kept his feelings close to the vest. Which, she'd come to realize, had been a smart choice. Emulating him had served her well as she'd been establishing herself as a no-nonsense hedge-fund analyst.

So why did he want to dredge up their past? Neither of them had made good choices, and that didn't need to be revisited.

The snipe about hero worship might have been overboard. As well as driving off on him while he was trying to respond.

But seriously! How else was a person supposed to react to getting pulled over and learning their ex was the officer in charge? Had he expected her to be *happy* while he ticketed her and implied she was the one who needed to open up?

She gritted her teeth, renewed anger heating her blood. Her peeling away while he was midsentence was a far smaller offense than him refusing to see her at the ranch. So he wanted to talk? Well, she'd been pregnant and desperate to talk then, and he hadn't been willing. She'd struggled through her miscarriage alone. And she didn't intend to bring it up now. Stella sighed. She didn't need one more unresolved thing hanging over her head, given the enormity of trying to earn her half siblings' forgiveness. To focus entirely on Lach, Maggie and Gramps tomorrow, she needed a clean slate. She could give Ryan two minutes to say whatever he needed to say. Him helping out at the work bee guaranteed they'd see each other again, so better do it now rather than have him pull her aside in the middle of a public gathering.

Flicking on her hazards, she slowed her car and pulled over again. He followed suit and jogged toward her car.

"Everything okay?" he asked as she rolled down the window.

She relaxed her clenched jaw. "Accusing you of wanting hero worship was a low blow," she admitted, shivering as a blast of cold air swept in. "Questionable ticket and sanctimony aside, you are quite the hero. So, thank you."

"Sanctimony?"

She pressed the home button on her phone. "Siri, define *sanctimony*."

"Oh, come on," Ryan snapped as the upper-crust English accent she'd chosen for her virtual assistant quoted the definition. "Moral superiority, Stella? That's rich."

She nodded her head in admission. "Maybe. Anyway, I only stopped to say thanks for what you did for Maggie."

He gripped the roof of the car with both hands. "I didn't do it for the accolades. I couldn't let you—" He shook his head. "Never mind."

"Me? What did it have to do with me?"

"Clearly, it didn't. Forget I said that."

How could she? Had he run into the fire for her somehow? "But—"

"Seriously. Leave it."

The flash of vulnerability on his face contradicted that tall, powerfully built frame of his. It might have been wintry outside, but her skin heated like she was lying on a towel in the Caribbean sun. He'd put on muscle over the years. *Not good.* She'd been sucked in by that tempting body before, with disastrous consequences.

About those... If you're being honest, you might as well—

No.

She wasn't about to bring up her miscarriage, not while snow was blowing into her car and he was standing with his gloved hands braced on the roof, dressed up like sex on a sheriff stick. Sucking in her bottom lip to keep from blurting something she didn't want to reveal, she fisted her hands on the wheel, needing the soft leather against her palms instead of the memory of gripping the hard plastic of a pregnancy test.

His eyes narrowed. "Was it that hard to say thank you, Stella?"

"What?"

Bemusement twisted the lips she'd kissed a thousand times. His voice was achingly soft for someone who had a belt full of weapons strapped around his lean hips. "You look pained."

"I'm fine." *Thank you* did not entail opening a vein. He'd made it clear he didn't want anything to do with her. "And I should have waited to say thanks until the work bee, when we're indoors. You look cold." He didn't, really. Despite the freezing temperatures, he looked plenty warm. And hot as sin, damn him.

Stop that. Think about the last time you were on this road with him.

Not hard to do, no matter how she'd tried to bury it. She'd be ninety and still able to feel the rain pattering on her cheeks, and the deep fear that her life had gone off the rails before she'd even pulled out of the station.

The life she'd built since had imploded on her, too. That was where her focus needed to be—regrouping, mending fences with her family and then salvaging her career. She'd wasted way too much time on this man, starting with the hours and days she'd cried over him after he refused to talk to her at the ranch. Good thing all that crying then had made her impervious to him now.

You wish.

He raked his hand down his face. His blue eyes were too damn earnest. They still held a hint of the devil-may-care boy he'd once been, but the faint crow's-feet reminded her that he'd done just as much living since high school as she had.

"It's really weird that you're here," he admitted gruffly.

It took everything she could not to react to his confession. "Water under the bridge."

His thinned lips suggested he knew she was lying, but he kept his thoughts to himself.

Thank God. "I think *sorry* and *thanks* are plenty for today—no need to go overboard on exchanging pleasantries."

"You and I have different definitions of *pleasant*." He cracked a smile. The jolt of it spread through her belly and settled between her legs.

That was one kind of pleasant they'd been darn good at, even as teenagers. *If only we'd been as good at making responsible decisions.*

He tipped the brim of his hat and strode back to his truck, leaving her to sit in the darkness of the unlit highway, heart in her throat.

She'd anticipated seeing Ryan, but not before she even arrived in town. And with him planning to help with barn construction, she'd be spending much more time with him than the "pass by on the street" encounters she'd prepared for. Between crossing the gulf between her and her siblings, and figuring out where she would land when she headed back to New York in two weeks, she had enough going on. She refused to add Ryan Rafferty to the list.

Ryan pulled up to his house and groaned when he saw the kitchen lights on. He'd told Stella the truth about not having a partner to come home to. But his grandmother had a key and absolutely no sense of personal space. He'd texted her earlier to ask her to feed his dog and let her out. He hadn't meant "stay until I get home."

Somewhere between pulling over Stella and turning onto his quiet street, he'd written off his plans to enjoy a glass of red wine with his feet up. He had two nights and a day until he'd be guaranteed to run into Stella again, and he needed to be well rested for whatever she threw his way at the work bee.

But he also had a hell of a time saying "no" to one Gertrude Rafferty. She'd been his rock during his childhood—after his mother had walked out when he was a toddler, his dad had made it clear mighty fast that he'd never wanted to be a parent. Ryan's gran had loved him enough for two people, and had done her best to shore him up when his dad's drug use disorder led to a fatal overdose.

Ryan was ever-thankful he'd won the grand-mother lottery. And by the mouthwatering smell of Bolognese sauce wafting from the kitchen, today was yet another example of that.

His stomach growled. Okay, eating was going to have to happen. As was casually telling his grand-mother that Stella was back in town. If Gran heard that he'd pulled over Stella from someone else, she'd consider it a personal insult.

He toed off his boots in his mudroom. His choc-olate Lab, Puddle, wagged her way over to him. He kneeled, taking a moment for a snuggle and to shower her with "good girl"s before heading into the kitchen.

Gran sat at the kitchen counter on a barstool, fid-dling with her tablet. With a backbone stiffer than the hairspray she still favored to keep her short sweep of now-gray hair in place, she had her thumb on the pulse of every living thing in Sutter Creek. Amazing she *hadn't* known Stella was coming to town, actually. But welcome. Better that he was the one to break the news.

"You didn't have to cook for me, Gran." He gave her a half hug and a kiss on top of her head.

"Ground round was on sale. There's enough for leftovers." She flipped the cover shut on her tablet and fixed him with a concerned look. "It's eleven o'clock. No wonder you can't keep a girlfriend. All these late nights... You look peaked."

He glanced up at the ceiling, tired of the common refrain. Of all people, she should understand how much it took to prove to everyone in Sutter Creek that he was worthy of their votes. He removed his duty belt and locked it away. After serving himself a heaping dish of pasta, he took a seat at the other barstool.

"Had an interesting roadside incident that delayed me more than expected," he said, trying to keep his voice mild.

"And?"

"You failed to tell me Stella Reid was coming back to town."

Silence followed, and a few blinks of disbelief. He couldn't tell whether she was shocked that she wasn't the first to know something, or felt guilty that she *had* known and hadn't given him a heads-up.

"Surprised?" he asked.

"Yes," she replied, cocking her head and pursing

her lips in disdain. "The last time I took Kittay in for a checkup, Tom said Stella was too busy at work to come for a visit. And given how much Tom sacrificed to come home, I wouldn't blame that man if he didn't want to speak to his granddaughter, let alone welcome her back into the fold."

Even after his brief retirement, Tom Reid still had the veterinary magic touch—Puddle loved her dog appointments. Tom was also way too kind to cut Stella out of his life.

"Tom's not the sort of guy who would blacklist one of his grandkids, Gran. And also…that sounds like a whole lot of 'not our business.'"

Her cheeks flushed. "Whatever you say. So, you were telling me about Stella. How is she?"

Prickly. Gorgeous. Still has a smile that makes my pulse skip.

"Fine," he said simply.

She poked him in the side. "*Fine?* The girl you intended to marry comes back to town and all you say is *fine*?"

"Let's not get carried away, there, Gran," he murmured. "We were only kids."

"What, you're going to deny I found a ring when I finally cleaned out your room before I moved to the seniors' facility?"

"One of many misguided choices of my youth. Laughable, to say the least. Or at least, it was at the time I bought that ring." *Do not let her think you're still soft for the woman.* "I was as infatuated as any eighteen-year-old boy would be. Key word—*was*."

"You took the fall for her. She should be thanking you."

"She did." Well, sort of. She'd thanked him for saving Maggie, and had admitted he'd done her a solid when he'd pretended she hadn't known the car was stolen. Put together—close enough.

She shook her head and tsked. "Stella Reid. And here I thought it was the cold and work stress putting that ruddy color in your cheeks."

He stared at his dinner so she wouldn't see the truth in his eyes. "We had a short conversation. Nothing more." But everything about the situation was sitting wrong. How he'd pushed her away so long ago, ignored her attempt to see him… It had seemed so crucial at the time, necessary as part of putting his life in order, in proving he wasn't going to go down the road his dad had traveled. But she was definitely still mad about it. And to hold on to something like that—Stella didn't seem the type. His well-honed cop radar twinged.

"Better not be more," Gran said. "She showed her colors when she let you get *arrested* for *her* crime."

"I was guilty, Gran. I deserved punishment."

"So did she."

"She'd never done anything like that before. Not like me." It hadn't been the first time he'd "borrowed" a vehicle without asking. He'd gone for more than one joyride, usually with his buddy Rafe

Brooks. It'd just taken stealing Ryan's unforgiving uncle's truck to finally get caught.

"Humph." Gran drummed her fingers on the counter. "You need someone who's as devoted to Sutter Creek as you are."

"Whoa, there. Who said anything about reconsidering what I had with Stella?" he grumbled.

"Your face said it for you."

"Seeing her bothered me, but not for the reasons you're thinking." He suspected he was part of the reason Stella had stayed away so long. Damn. Just when he was starting to think he was truly clear of his mistakes—getting elected sheriff was supposed to have proven that—another painful reminder surfaced.

"Just be careful." Pointing a finger at him, she warned, "She was your first love. We get nostalgic about that."

"I'm not feeling nostalgic."

"You're feeling *something*."

He'd let Gran see too much. Holy hell, this was embarrassing. Hiding his emotions was part of his job. He'd faced down criminals with no hint of what he was feeling. But combine Stella and Gran, and he was apparently as expressive as an overeager community-theater actor.

Ryan tucked in to the rest of his dinner, mind whirling. He'd have to make sure that he didn't let the same thing happen at work tomorrow. He had a meeting with the mayor and the head of the local ranching association about a recent rash of cattle thefts, and if either of them clued in that he was distracted, he'd be facing questions about Stella that he definitely didn't want to answer.

Chapter Four

Stella's phone dinged right when she was finishing flat-ironing her hair the next morning. The primping might have been overkill, but it never hurt to show up ready for anything. She planned to fetch coffee to take to Lachlan and Maggie as a peace offering, and who knew whom she'd run into on Main Street. Her pride wouldn't let her look anything less than her best. A little "check out what I've done with my life" jab.

Ugh. How was it she'd been in Sutter Creek for less than twelve hours and was already worrying about what everyone thought of her? It wasn't high school anymore, and she needed to put on her grown-ass woman pants and stop thinking as if it was.

Putting down the styling wand, she checked her phone.

Her stomach turned. The notification screen was going berserk. There were numerous texts from work, and emails from three reporters who all wanted her take on the rumors. *Freaking great.*

A dropped call from a Montana number she didn't recognize sat sandwiched between all the work crap. *Weird.* Well, she wasn't in the mood to talk to anyone who wasn't one of her half siblings, and they would have called her from their own numbers.

Stella put down the device. She'd check the voice mail later.

And she'd leave the texts and emails, too. Everything going on in New York could wait. It *had to* wait. She had explicit orders not to talk to *anyone*, let alone colleagues or reporters. Today was for coffee bribery, and some more lying to Lachlan and Maggie about why she'd essentially ghosted them. Exhaustion pressed on her shoulders, and she took a deep breath. Being Friday, she knew they'd be working, so she'd meet them at the clinic. She preferred that, honestly. She had way too many memories of crying on the couch at her grandparents' old place, where Maggie now lived.

The barn's behind the clinic, though. And the loft was an aching reminder of her stolen moments with Ryan. Fumbling fingers and clumsy caresses—all that teenage fervor. Love, too. The crash and burn had been devastating, but what came before it… She sure hadn't felt anything similar in any of her dating forays in Manhattan.

She put her phone away and threw on her coat and boots. Priority one: caffeine. Mental armor via espresso bean before she faced talking to her siblings about her current problems. Her decision to stay at a hotel last night might have infuriated Lachlan, but who knew how things would have gone had she shown up? She probably would have said or done the wrong thing and made him even angrier than she had by refusing his spare bedroom. And the Sutter Mountain Hotel had been an opulent place to land last night.

An added benefit? One hundred percent less family drama.

Her conscience didn't let her sit with that satisfaction for long.

Right. One hundred percent more sibling guilt. Would she ever figure out how to be an acceptable sister?

Heading out of the glitzy lobby into the January morning, she jammed her hands into her thin, knit gloves to fend off the cold. Giant logs served as portico supports on either side of her, grand enough to stand up to the view of the mountain in front. The sky was as blue as it could possibly be. Snow from last night's storm crunched under her heeled boots, a carpet of white around the base lift near the resort hotel. A far cry from the dingy slush lining Manhattan's streets.

Point: Montana.

Gritting her teeth at the begrudging admission of superiority, she trudged down the path connecting her hotel and the center of town. Trees lined either side of the path, muting the noise from nearby streets, and a layer of icing-sugar snow dusted the thick, green branches.

Awareness crawled up the back of her neck. Since when did she find towering trees more eye-catching than soaring skyscrapers? She lived for New York's "the city that never sleeps" vibe and the enthralling architecture. And, sure, she liked being on first-name basis with the owner of the bodega on the corner of her block, but she didn't need him to know her life story. She'd experienced enough neighborly "concern" before she moved away from Sutter Creek to last a lifetime.

She rounded the corner of the path to the town center, where four streets of buildings framed what was a big lawn during the summer. Today, snow covered the wide expanse. A pine tree as tall as the two-story buildings surrounding the square shaded a gazebo and a jelly-bean-shaped ice rink. At Christmastime, the tree was decorated with lights and a star, but any trace of last month's holiday was long gone.

"Place hasn't changed much," she muttered to herself. Except, she had to admit there were a lot of differences. Sure, Ryan's family's bakery was there, windows painted with a cupcake logo and Sweets and Treats in pink, flowing script, but a number of restaurants existed that hadn't before. Far more high-end amenities for tourists—spas and shops—but without erasing the town's ranching roots. Most of the buildings, freshly painted in cheery pastels, had the Old West fronts she remembered from her teen years. It was…pretty. *Huh.* Quaint and homey, not suffocating and backward like she remembered.

And the fresh air, untainted by exhaust and questionable air-vent smells, was like taking a giant pipe cleaner to the lungs. Maybe she needed to walk the few blocks to Central Park more once she was back home. She'd certainly have time, unless the authorities sped up the criminal-charges process.

A bunch of elementary-age kids skated around the rink, a school group by the looks of it. A peanut of a girl twirled on the ice, totally in the "dreaming of being an Olympic figure skater" zone. Stella halted on the path that cut through the snow-covered lawn to watch. The pint-size skater dipped her head back and spun with her arms extended. Stella's heart panged. She missed that special freedom of twirling on skates. She'd taken skating lessons as a kid, had even competed for a few years until it got too expensive to buy skates and ice time and private coaching. Her mom's refusal to take any sort of child support from Stella's father had put a damper on Stella's utterly unlikely chance at Olympic fame.

"Taking you back?"

She startled at the gruff interruption. Peering at

her intruder out of the corner of her eye, she replied, "Little bit."

Two words was about all she could get out. Her mouth dried up so fast, it was like she'd stuffed a towel in it. Ryan in uniform in the daylight was sanity-stealing. It shouldn't have been. Black jacket, tan pants—nothing special. Law-enforcement officers had never been her jam. But something about the way his jacket stretched across his broad shoulders made her want to put a hand there for a second—test just how much stronger he'd gotten since she last wrapped her arms around him.

Admit it, it's the cowboy hat.

Damn it, what was she doing? Ryan was not hers to admire, hadn't been since she was barely old enough to vote. And he was still the same guy under the badge. A person couldn't change that much.

"Excuse me. I was headed to get coffee." Forcing a smile, she backed away and hurried toward Peak Beans, the café nestled between a sporting-goods store and an upscale esthetician's salon.

Ryan caught up to her right before she got to the street. "Stella, slow down."

"What? I'm not jaywalking. It's pedestrian-only."

He smiled ruefully. "I'm not here to police your behavior. I'm just coincidentally also in need of joe. I just finished up at the ATM—" he pointed across the square at the brick front of the bank, then gestured past Main Street at a partly visible, glass-sided structure glinting in the morning sun "—before going to my office."

"Right," she grumbled, opening the door to the coffee shop and lining up behind the half-dozen sleepy-looking people who were also in need of a pick-me-up. Vintage-ski chic added a cozy ambiance to the place. A garland of jewel-toned pom-poms was draped along the barn-wood counter. A chalkboard filled the wall behind, displaying the menu, and hand-drawn marmots skied down the border next to the prices. Apparently, the town mascot hadn't changed.

Most tables were occupied. A few faces looked a bit familiar, but many weren't. Tourists, probably. And a reminder of how she'd spent her high-school years with one foot out the door—she'd kept to herself, so she hadn't bothered to maintain connections over social media.

"How was your hotel?" Ryan asked.

She didn't hear any judgment over not staying with a family member in his tone. "Quieter than staying at Lachlan's. And Maggie already has Gramps with her."

He let out a dissatisfied sound in his throat.

Yeah, *there* was the guilt trip. *I'm well capable of guilting myself without your help, Ryan.* She was about to say just that when the college-age barista behind the counter asked him if he wanted his usual order.

"Yes, thanks," he replied. "And a—" His eyebrows knitted. "What do you want, Stella? Still a vanilla latte drinker?"

Heat infused her cheeks. "I can buy my own coffee, thanks."

He sighed. "Suit yourself. Where are you off to this morning?"

"The clinic. I'm going to take Lachlan and Maggie some java and catch up with them."

Ryan looked puzzled. "Aren't they doing search-and-rescue training this morning? The team's practicing a joint exercise with the mountain crew."

She blinked. "Not that I know of."

Lachlan wouldn't have double-booked on purpose, would he?

Maybe he *would* have, given how livid he'd been. Had he been her early unknown caller? She pulled out her cell and showed Ryan the alert. "Do you recognize this number?"

He nodded. "It's the staff line at the mountain's safety and risk management office."

She winced. The voice mail probably was from Lach.

A quick check of the message confirmed that her half siblings were busy until the afternoon. Lach also pointed out that their grandfather, who was still covering for Maggie on most of the veterinary work, was working that morning.

Wow. Canceling via voice mail. Talk about taking a page out of her own book.

"They stood me up," she mumbled.

"Not exactly," he said. "One of them called you."

"Lach did. But he could have told me last night." Now she was going to be spinning her wheels in town for the morning.

I deserve it. Had she really expected them to roll out the red carpet for her with how she'd treated them over the past six months? Though her brother and Marisol had tried, she supposed, with the bathroom cleaning and changing the sheets.

Her stomach soured, and the coffee and pastry scents of the shop became overly strong. "He must be angrier with me than I thought."

Ryan narrowed his eyes. "Have you seen Laura yet?"

He knew full well she hadn't. Her face heated. "No. That's another reason why I'm here."

"She's a sweetheart."

The underside of her tongue pinched. If she hadn't lost their baby and had decided to carry it to term, they'd have a teenager on their hands. She hadn't been able to picture Ryan as a father then. Hell, he'd claimed he didn't want to be one many a time while talking about his own dad. But the man in front of her, with his protective stance and shoulders wide enough to hold up the world… "Since when do you like kids?"

"Since I grew up, Stella. Not sure why you're so intent on defining me by my teenage mistakes, but I guess that'll happen when the last mistake I made was a pretty monstrous one."

Her cheeks chilled and she swallowed the lump in her throat. "Yeah, well, it's a habit."

He jerked his head in affirmation. "Laura will steal your heart in a second. She did mine."

Seriously? He lets babies steal his heart now? "I—I'm sure she will," she said. "Unfortunately, work meant not being able to get away."

"Not even to see your *niece*?"

"It's a long story."

"Family should always—" The barista called Ryan up. "Excuse me," he said, striding to the counter.

Stella uttered silent thanks that he hadn't finished his thought. He seemed to have far too many opinions on her relationship with her siblings.

She loved Maggie and Lachlan. And she'd been proud of them from afar. Both successful business owners, both in healthy relationships.

Since learning about the fire, Stella had also discovered Maggie was head over heels for Sutter Creek's new librarian and his young daughter. *Boyfriend* and *Maggie* were two words she'd never thought would go together. Her sister had never dated someone long enough to use that label, not until Asher and Ruth had worked their way into Maggie's heart. And thankfully for Lachlan, Marisol's surprise pregnancy had a far happier ending than Stella's. He was engaged to the mother of his child, and they were cozied up in a little house—

Ryan's grandmother's old place, for God's sake—establishing their lives together.

But dealing with the repercussions of faulty contraception was a hell of a lot different at thirtysomething than at eighteen. Stella hadn't even processed being pregnant before she miscarried. A good thing, really—she'd been way too young.

And the man over at the cream-and-sugar bar, calmly doctoring his brew with a dollop from the small, stainless-steel container labeled 2% milk, had no idea about any of it. What would he say if she told him now? If she filled him in on why she'd come to see him at the ranch that day?

Stop it. Just don't go there. Digging up old emotions would only distract her from getting her family put back to rights and finding a new place to land professionally.

Ryan returned to her side right after she put in her order for a sugar-free vanilla latte.

"I remembered correctly," he said smugly.

She lifted a shoulder and shuffled over to an empty spot at the end of the counter, where a chalkboard had "pick up" written on it in rainbow lettering. "You always had a good memory. Being smart probably comes in handy now." She waved at the sheriff insignia on his jacket.

"I was stupid about many, many things. But I've earned this badge, Stella. You didn't see it, being gone. But if you'd give me the chance, I could…" He cleared his throat.

She lifted an eyebrow, ignoring how the thickness in his voice sent pangs of something ricocheting through her chest.

Motioning for him to elaborate, she prompted, "Could…?"

"Make it up to you somehow. How about I start by giving you a ride to the clinic this afternoon? I was planning to head out to talk to Lachlan and Maggie later today, anyway."

"The last time I got a ride with you, my life went to hell," she said, unable to stop a smile at the black humor of his invitation.

He reddened. "Christ, I—"

She waved a hand. "I was actually kind of kidding."

His jaw dropped.

She pressed her lips together, her surprise matching his. When had she ever managed anything close to laughing at that night? There was nothing funny about what they'd done. Stealing his uncle's pride and joy, an antique pickup with an immaculate, cherry-red paint job. It hadn't been so immaculate after Stella tried to kiss Ryan while driving and ended up scraping that telephone pole…

"Don't you have an entire county to supervise?" she groused, accepting her drink from the barista and taking as large a slurp as she could without burning the roof of her mouth. "Maybe they need you in West Yellowstone or something."

He eyed her, his smile knowing. "I manage to be where I'm needed, Stella."

"Must be a new skill then." The bitter comment slipped out before she could stop it. *Oh, crap.*

"Yeah, it is," he said. He motioned for her to go ahead of him as they left the café. "I wouldn't have been elected sheriff if I wasn't responsible."

"Right. Well." She took a deep breath. "You go be responsible. I'll be fine."

He cupped her shoulder and stroked it with his thumb. Sparks shimmied down her arm—

Oh, good *grief*! How was that still possible?

"Fine?" he repeated gruffly. "You sure?"

"Obviously." She shifted away from his touch, the urge to confess her troubles bubbling to the surface. Stupid latent habit, wanting to use him as a sounding board. *It worked* so *well last time you tried.*

"And I get you not telling me your secrets. But I *am* a trained investigator. I could figure them out." Winking, he nodded a farewell and ambled down the street.

Blood rushed from her limbs. Was he seriously going to look into her life? He wouldn't find evidence of her miscarriage. Only Lach and Maggie knew about it, and they wouldn't tell. But if he started poking around, would her record show that she was working with the fraud investigation? What if other people in the sheriff's office saw him doing it and learned the details before they were supposed to go public? The way news spread around Sutter Creek, if one person knew, everyone would. And not only did her NDA require silence, it was also humiliating as anything to have people see that she'd trusted the wrong person. Again.

Damn it. She needed to control what he found out to prevent it from spreading elsewhere. Good thing he hadn't gotten far, what with his easy, strolling pace.

"Wait!" She jogged after him, her heels clicking on the board sidewalks. "Don't investigate me. Please."

Ryan turned around slowly, Stella's rapid footsteps reverberating through him. Panic splotched her cheeks pink.

He glanced to his left, peeking around the giant cupcake painted on the plate-glass window. His aunt Nancy was watching him from behind the counter of the family bakery. She lifted a hand in a wave and an eyebrow in curiosity. He waved back and motioned for Stella to follow him over in front of the next store. Having a conversation in the line at Peak Beans was one thing, but his former flame being agitated right in front of Sweets and Treats was another. He'd be dealing with phone calls all afternoon if Gran was inside helping out.

Stella hurried to follow him. Her hands clutched her to-go cup—it was the grip of a person struggling to hold it together. The desperation twisting her lips piqued his curiosity even more. Small circles marked the skin under her eyes, even though she was wearing makeup. Maybe her claim that it was more restful to stay at a hotel than at Lachlan's had been a lie. Whatever her reasons, the thought of him looking into her life was upsetting her, which hadn't been his intent.

"I was kidding, Stella. It's not ethical for me to go poking around in someone's records without cause."

A little color faded from her cheeks. "Crappy joke, Sheriff."

"Maybe so. But now I'm actually wondering what's wrong." Which was not where his focus needed to be thirty minutes before meeting with the mayor and the head of the county ranching association.

"So you *are* going to look into my record?"

"Do I need to?"

"No. I didn't do anything wrong, but—" She rubbed her face with one of her gloved hands.

His inner problem solver clamored for answers. *Not now.* He needed to get to the office and deal with work before he could worry about Stella. She'd already delayed him enough.

Covering the intensity of his curiosity by sipping his coffee, he swallowed and said, "Though that *but* intrigues me, I have a meeting I need to get to."

Her face crumpled. "Please leave it be."

"You're sure you're not in trouble?"

She nodded sharply.

He didn't believe that for a second—only a threat put that fearful expression on a person's face—but he didn't have enough of a reason to investigate, no matter how concerned he was. No matter how strong the need to protect her that settled, unwanted, in his belly. "Not my business then, Stella."

She exhaled and took a few backward steps. "Thanks. See you later."

"Oh, likely. Excuse me while I head for my meeting."

Step one: stop watching her cross the square.

Necessary, but almost painful to follow through on. Man, she created a picture—those long legs in tight jeans and sexy boots. Tearing his gaze from the alluring sight, he spun and hurried in the direction of his workplace, narrowly avoiding a collision with one of his grandmother's good friends.

"What on earth—"

"Sorry, Mrs. Brooks," he called, continuing before the older woman could question the reason for his lack of attention. Two minutes later, he strode into the airy foyer of the emergency-services building and waved at the receptionist, who was holding court with a couple of firefighters. His department shared the building with the firefighters and paramedics, which made for convenient interdepartmental dealings, but with a side effect of being gossip central. He did not have time to be the center of the conversation, and by the way the group was looking at him with interest, news of Stella's arrival had traveled mighty fast.

"Heard you pulled over an interesting car last

night, Sheriff," Graydon Halloran, the town's youngest firefighter called out, a pot-stirring smile on his face.

Ryan narrowed his eyes and paused with his hand on the door that led to his department's space. "Since when do you have access to the computer records, Halloran?"

"I don't. Who needs technology when your grandma's around? She was talking to my mom. Who kindly brought me breakfast and all sorts of questions about your dating life."

The back of Ryan's neck prickled. Graydon Halloran's mom was the very rancher he was about to meet with. She'd put her clout as a local cattle maven behind him in the last election, a critical step for his campaign success. If it wasn't for Georgie Halloran and her brother, whose family owned Sutter Mountain Resort, he wouldn't be sheriff. He'd have to make sure she knew Stella's return to town wasn't going to affect his commitment to the county one iota.

"I'm well aware my grandmother keeps the gossip chain greased," he said. "I just didn't think she would work so damn fast. It isn't even ten o'clock."

But Sweets and Treats opened at six, and Gran was used to waking up early from having owned and run the place until she was in her early seventies. She made harassing his aunts a regular part of her week. Which meant she must have been talking up Stella's visit while doing her morning rounds. Christ. *Had* she seen them talking on the sidewalk just now? If so, he'd never let him hear the end of it.

"My mom's in your office," Graydon said. "Probably waiting to grill you worse than she just did me."

"She's here *already*?" Ryan checked the clock on the wall behind the receptionist. He had ten minutes until the meeting was supposed to start, and he always liked being the first to arrive.

Swearing under his breath, he dismissed the group at the reception desk with a wave and pushed through the door.

Deputy Wayne Ross leaned against the counter lining one side of the space. He stirred his coffee with a wooden stir stick, watching Ryan, and lifted his graying eyebrows. "You sure know how to roll out the welcome mat, Sheriff. Woulda thought you'd have given Stella a break for old time's sake."

Ryan hurried past, weaving through the work stations dividing the open-concept space. "We agreed that stretch of highway needed extra attention, Wayne. And I didn't initially know Stella was driving. She was in a rental."

"Not the first time she's been pulled over in someone else's vehicle," the deputy quipped.

Turning to fix Wayne with a glare, Ryan said, "No point in bringing that up."

"Tell that to Miz Georgie in there." Wayne gestured at Ryan's office with his World's Best Grandpa mug. "She's on a mission of some sort."

The eggs Ryan had eaten for breakfast churned in

his stomach. Fixing an impervious expression on his face, he entered his office. The tension he felt eased off a little when he saw Georgie was alone; the mayor hadn't arrived yet. But her concerned expression was enough to have him tasting bacon.

"Georgie Halloran, what can I do you for?"

The woman sat in one of the chairs surrounding the four-person table he kept opposite his desk. She was white and nearing sixty, but looked a decade younger. Her long, dark brown hair was pulled off her tanned face in a no-nonsense ponytail, and she wore a plain blouse and jeans with cowboy boots that were far more on the working end of the style spectrum. She reminded him of Stella's sister, Maggie, that way. Stella, on the other hand, had been in her all-black, urban getup this morning. Nothing near what she should be wearing to clean up a burned-down barn. Maggie would set her straight, get her in something more appropriate. *Something equally hot...*

"Close the door, Sheriff," Georgie said briskly. "I know you've got some new developments to keep that mind of yours racing, and I want to throw a few thoughts into the mix for you to mull over."

Heat rushed up the back of his neck at having been caught on the verge of daydreaming. *Focus, Rafferty. Georgie Halloran is more important to your future than Stella will ever be.*

"I'm not late, am I?" he asked, keeping his tone light. He hung his jacket on the coatrack in the corner and took a seat across from her, adjusting his duty belt as he settled into the chair. "Meeting's at ten?"

"This isn't about the cattle theft."

"No?"

Her expression softened. Given her daughters were older than Graydon and fairly close in age to Ryan, her motherly gaze suited the age gap between Georgie and him. But this wasn't their normal dynamic. The only person in the world who'd ever mothered him was his grandmother.

"Your aunt's croissants were on point this morning," she said. "Worthy bakery visit."

He tilted his head. "I know police officers are stereotyped for their love of baked goods, but—"

"I need you to promise me you're not going to up and move to New York on me, Ryan."

"Ah." He sat back in his chair and took a drink from his to-go cup. "Figured you were here about Stella."

"I remember you back then. Her, too." Sadness flickered across her face. "And I know what I've invested in you now. You have a heart for this community. And Stella Reid doesn't."

"All fairly irrelevant, Georgie. Our relationship since she left has consisted of a roadside conversation and a chance encounter in a coffee line. Both within the last twelve hours."

Both of which knocked me on my ass.

She nodded, crossing her arms. "Your grandmother looked worried this morning. I wanted to see for myself that she was off base. You severed your connection with Stella too long ago for it to cause problems for you now."

"Right you are. And know I'm one hundred percent focused on Sutter Creek's well-being."

Guilt swamped him. Such a lie. Less than a day of Stella being in town, and he couldn't get her off his mind. He hated to think of what he'd be like two weeks from now.

"As soon as the mayor gets here, Georgie, I'll show you how and why I don't have room in my life for anything except for the safety of our community."

"You don't need to be a monk, Ryan. Balance is key. Find yourself a local woman, someone who cares for Sutter Creek like you do." Her frown bent into a crafty smile. "You know, you should consider asking Emma out. She's career-driven, just like you. The two of you could distract each other from your long hours."

He shook his head. Wasn't the first time someone had tried to set him up with one of Georgie's daughters, and it wasn't the first time he'd say no. "Emma and I don't have that special spark, Georgie. Sorry to disappoint."

He was distracted enough by the only woman with whom he *had* discovered that special spark. The woman he most needed to keep at arm's length now, if he was going to keep his life in the direction he'd been aiming it for years.

A knock sounded on the door. It opened, and

Wayne stuck his head in. "Sheriff? Feds are on the line. Want them patched through to your cell?"

Georgie's eyes lit up. "Concerning the thefts?"

"Let me see, and I'll let you know if I can tell you," Ryan said. Wanting privacy without kicking Georgie out, he excused himself and went to the conference room next door. He answered his phone the second it rang. "Ryan Rafferty."

"Sheriff Rafferty. Special Agent Rishi Gill here. Thanks for taking my call."

"Sure." As much as he loved investigations, the FBI had interstate abilities he did not. "Glad we finally made it on your radar. I've been trying to get federal interest in our cattle thefts for—"

"Gonna stop you there, Rafferty. I'm in the white-collar crime division, not cows."

Ryan stilled. This reeked of complications. "Not 'cows.' Got it. Do we have a different problem?"

"Maybe. I believe you know Stella Reid?"

Stella was mixed up with the FBI? Why? Heart suddenly in his throat, he croaked, "Yeah. She's a… family friend."

"She's also a witness of mine. An informant in a securities fraud case at her firm. And it's not procedure for me to involve you. Counting on you not telling anyone I did, in fact. But—I like Stella. She's good people."

"Do you suspect anyone will follow her here?"

"To the middle of nowhere? No. It's why we let her leave New York. But she's been through the wringer since she blew the whistle on her boss. If anyone caused problems for her and I hadn't at least alerted you to the situation, I'd feel responsible."

"Uh, wow." Gran would have told Ryan to close his mouth because he was catching flies, but this wasn't your average news. A criminal investigation at a hedge fund? And Stella was the informant? That'd make the national news when it got out. "So this is just a courtesy call? Or do you need something specific from me?"

"Not unless there's an issue. She's under an NDA. Won't be saying anything."

God, poor Stella. Explained why she hadn't been home for a visit since Laura was born. "Got it. I'll keep an eye on anything suspicious."

He signed off with Agent Gill and returned to his office. His mind buzzed. A federal investigation was a lot to carry for anyone, especially having to keep it to herself. Impressive that Stella wasn't a basket case.

And it made her earlier plea that he not investigate her make so much more sense. She wouldn't want the FBI to think she'd broken her NDA.

"Sheriff?" Georgie Halloran still sat at the table. Her curious gaze drilled into him. "Was it the FBI? Are they getting involved in your investigation?"

He shook off his fog. "'Fraid I can't say, Georgie. But if the feds were getting involved, it wouldn't be a secret."

She visibly deflated. "Damn. I had such hopes."

"I know. I'll keep working on it." Making progress on that case was critical. So was ensuring Stella was safe, though. He intended to keep more than an eye on her like he'd promised Agent Gill. But he'd have to be careful. Her involvement would inevitably go public. Depending on how the story got framed, if Stella's ethics or actions were called into question, and he was linked to her, even the appearance of condoning unethical business practices could reflect poorly on him.

The town had forgiven him once for his mistakes. They probably wouldn't again.

Chapter Five

Stella stared at the boarded-over barn windows, heart catching in her throat. Each sheet of plywood was a reminder of how close she, Lach and Gramps had been to losing Maggie. *Wow.* She'd seen the insurance pictures of the sooty and charred interior, and had followed the progress of the restoration company. But witnessing the wreckage in person made her eyes sting.

It was a stark reminder of what *could* have happened.

A dry sob climbed up Stella's throat. But before it could escape, a cranky complaint came from behind her, jarring her.

"If you'd given us more than two days' notice,

we'd have been able to make our excuses at SAR training."

The snarky tone grounded Stella in the here and now, where both her half siblings were alive and well and freaking pissed at her.

She whirled to face Maggie. Alive Maggie. Breathing Maggie.

Irritated-as-hell Maggie.

Short blond curls pinned back haphazardly, confirming they'd been styled by someone who couldn't properly hold a comb, Maggie glanced away from both Stella and the building. She crossed her arms over the half-zip fleece jacket she wore with fitted sweatpants and hiking boots. Knitted mittens covered her hands, making it impossible for Stella to take stock of Maggie's ongoing recovery from her burns. Surely she still had bandages on, given her most recent plastic surgery had only been a couple of weeks ago.

Silence stretched until an uncomfortable shiver ran down Stella's limbs. Crap, right, it was her turn to respond. Maggie had thrown out that barb about the short notice, and was obviously waiting for Stella to make an excuse.

"I came the minute I could get away," she explained.

"The four months we've waited for you to come visit your niece would call you a liar." Maggie squeezed her eyes shut for a second.

"I'm sorry." Guilt washed over Stella. "Really."

Maggie studied her. "So you say." Her gaze flicked to the barn. "You looking for a tour or something?"

Stella shook her head. "I thought I should face down our demons before the work bee."

"*Our* demons?"

"Yeah. We almost lost you."

"I definitely put us into scramble mode. Extra money for a locum to cover until Gramps could get home. Turning Gramps's life on its head. And the delays for Lachlan…"

"Lachlan's delays weren't your doing. Take the blame for your injuries all you want, but not for the fire itself." The fire had started when Maggie's boyfriend's daughter had tried to warm up Lachlan's office one afternoon and had turned on a space heater that malfunctioned. After initially leaving the burning building with Asher and his daughter, Maggie had run back in to save a backpack full of family letters for the young girl. The aftermath—Maggie's burned hands, their grandfather moving back from Arizona and stepping back in as veterinarian—had required a lot of juggling. "No, erase that. *Blame* isn't the right word. You made a judgment call. You don't need to regret that."

Or so she'd been telling herself since she picked up the phone and called the SEC hotline six months ago. She'd never regret keeping her integrity, much like she doubted her sister would change her decision to run in after Asher's daughter's letters. But both decisions came with some heavy-ass consequences.

"I guess," Maggie said, and held out her arms. "Welcome back."

Oh. Well, then. Not the animosity she was expecting.

Pushing down the impulse to remind Maggie she was only here for a short visit, Stella accepted her sister's offered hug. Maggie was six inches shorter, and with her hiking boots, compared to Stella's heeled ones, she just cleared Stella's chin. Her sister smelled like fresh air, which was probably her usual, but it had been so long since they hugged that it stuck out.

"How did you manage to do a SAR exercise so soon after surgery?" Stella asked.

"Strictly on the sidelines." Maggie backed up and took off a mitten, displaying the gauze wrapped around the palm and half her fingers. "It's why I'm back before noon. Lach stayed to finish up, but I couldn't go into the out-of-bounds areas. I have to be careful with my graft work."

"And Gramps is seeing patients?"

Judgment flickered across Maggie's face. "You haven't gone in to say hi?"

She shook her head. "It's been a while since I've seen him. I'd rather not have an audience."

Maggie rolled her eyes. "Life doesn't have to be so complicated, Stella. Just break the seal. Hell, you did it with Ryan already."

"How do you know?"

"The sheriff pulls his high-school sweetheart over on the highway? That's solid coffee-break fodder, especially for the SAR crew. We work closely with Ryan. And if you managed to get through an encounter with him, you'd think our grandfather would be easy in comparison."

She winced. Maggie had a point, but it was just as hard to face her family. She actually wanted a relationship with them, so a bit more broken-glass-walking was required. "I texted Gramps, letting him know I'd be here when he was done for the day."

"What, you're going to wait around an hour, lurking outside until he's finished?"

"I wasn't sure when everyone would be free."

"Good grief. Just come to my house."

"But—" *It's easier to avoid thinking about Ryan if I avoid your house.*

"No *buts*. Come make me lunch. I've been feeling badly for relying on Asher so much, and I refused his help before he left for work. All I managed was microwave oatmeal."

Right. It was either admit to Maggie that she had unresolved feelings about her high-school breakup, or go along and be helpful.

She clapped her hands once. "Fine. Lunch it is."

Maggie led the way across the road to the ranch that had been their grandparents' prior to Maggie stepping into approximately eight pairs of their grandfather's shoes. Their grandmother had passed away years ago, and Gramps had finally retired when Maggie had finished the process of buying the clinic.

They entered the house through the side entrance into the kitchen. Some things were still the same: the wooden table surrounded by a mix of spindle-back chairs had been one of their grandmother's famous thrift-store finds, as had the mismatched collection of knobs on the white cabinetry. But Maggie had updated the walls from wallpaper to a soft yellow paint.

"What, the avocado-green appliances had to go? Say it ain't so," Stella said.

Maggie laughed, and the pressure in Stella's chest eased a little. Her sister didn't seem as angry as Lachlan. But, then, it wasn't Maggie's child that she hadn't managed to meet in person yet.

"Coffee?" Her sister moved to fill the carafe.

"Sit," Stella commanded, pointing at the kitchen table. A pile of kids' artwork and a box of markers sat beside the antique salt and pepper mills that had passed through the family for generations. The homey kitsch was nothing like the sleek white and gray lines of her NYC apartment.

The few friends she ever invited into her place hinted at it being sterile. But why fuss with decorating? She spent so much time at the office, her apartment was more like a hotel room. Was she missing out on something by not having personal touches? Shoving down her doubt, she focused on the assortment of markers. "So, uh, Asher and his daughter are living here?"

Maggie shook her head, a dreamy look crossing her face.

"Wow, look at you, all in love. I don't think I've ever seen you wear that expression."

"Hard to get a good sample size when we see each other all of once a year. If that," Maggie grumbled.

"I guess, yeah," she admitted. She refilled the water reservoir in the coffee maker, topped up the grounds basket and set it to brew.

Even before she'd been required to stay in New York for investigation purposes, keeping her distance from Sutter Creek had seemed logical. She'd never felt fully a part of her family, and her mom's hostility over her father's infidelity had created division. And that bitterness had made it too easy to resent the town.

Her mom had hated living in Sutter Creek but hadn't seen a way out, being a single parent with only a year of college under her belt. She'd worked at a diner on the outskirts of town, busting her butt for tips and being too stubborn to accept alimony from Stella's dad, even though he easily could have afforded it out of his generous lawyer's salary. When Stella was in college, her mom had waited on a table of tourists and started dating one of the men, and soon after had moved to San Diego. She'd drilled truth into Stella at a young age: Sutter Creek would hold her back from happiness and success.

So why did I also *manage to crash and burn in the heart of Wall Street?*

Nor did the impact of her self-imposed isolation sit well anymore. She was only a visitor in Maggie's kitchen. A guest, not a fixture.

Sighing, she poured Maggie a coffee and gestured to the pad of doodled-on paper. "Asher and Ruth are here a lot, even if they don't live here?"

"Yeah. We've been going back and forth between his place and mine since the fire. It's a bit weird to be cohabitating under the supervision of a ten-year-old and a septuagenarian. But it's not like I have a choice." Maggie studied the gauze strips wrapped around her hands. Her happy smile crumbled. "I need the help. I'm eternally thankful that I have Asher, and that he's willing to support me, but it's a really big burden for him to have to do everything for me *and* Ruth…" Wiping at her eyes, she made a face. "I hate feeling helpless."

"It's your job to heal, which means rest. Naps and accepting that people show they love you by doing things for you—" *And I've done the opposite.*

Maggie looked stricken. Her hand shook as she lifted her mug to her lips.

A lump filled Stella's throat. She swallowed a few times to get her voice back. "Lunch. Tell me what to do."

"Sandwiches are fine." Her sister pointed at the fridge and a bread box with two half-bent fingers. "So Ryan actually gave you a ticket last night?"

"No mercy. The jerk."

Maggie sighed and fiddled with the edge of one

of her dressings. "They've been ticketing like crazy on the highway since a college kid died last month when he drove off the road and hit a tree."

"That's awful. He didn't mention that... But still. I was barely over the speed limit."

"You know, I was really happy to dislike Ryan forever for what he did to you. But then he pulled me out of the fire. Plus, I have to admit he's a good sheriff. I've felt like a traitor, easing up on him."

"He saved your life. You're allowed." She plucked ingredients for turkey sandwiches from the fridge.

"He did." Maggie's eyes glinted with moisture. "But refusing to talk to you back then, and feeling so freaking helpless when you miscarried... It's been hard not to ream him out for that a thousand times."

Stella sliced the cheese too hard, and the knife hit the cutting board with a thunk. Steadying her hands, she said, "Please don't. Had I actually ended up with a baby, I would have pushed harder for him to listen. But I didn't need to."

"I guess."

"And what good will it do either of us to hash out what could have been?"

Maggie shrugged. "Depends on how much you're over it."

"I'm totally over it!"

"Right."

Yeah, Stella wouldn't have believed that protest, either.

"It was eighteen years ago." She finished constructing Maggie's sandwich, threw it on a plate and placed it on the table.

Her sister took a bite and chewed thoughtfully.

"What?" Stella said, far sharper than she'd intended. She jammed the ingredients back in the fridge, then bent to get ice from the back of one of the freezer drawers. Her coffee this morning had made her jittery enough—she'd be better off with water.

Maggie snorted. "You tell me."

"Well, I—"

A creak sounded through the door to the dining room and living room. Two sets of heavy footsteps plunked toward the kitchen.

"Gramps! Lach," she called, juggling the ice-cube tray.

"Stella?" her brother greeted, voice gruff.

"Hey, Stella."

Not her grandfather's voice.

She shot to her feet, fumbling to close the freezer with a toe. She clung to the fridge to stay upright. Her weight jarred the appliance, and a couple of Maggie's Grumpy Cat magnets clattered to the pine-colored laminate.

Both men's eyebrows rose. Ryan's in concern; Lachlan's, more like brotherly disdain.

"Forgot how to stand, Stell?" Lachlan asked. He looked good. His tawny hair was windblown, and the beard he'd grown since the fall added to his ruggedness. He wore an outdoorsy getup similar to Maggie's. A few lines etched his eyes—the mark of a man with an infant at home—but he was fit as ever and carried an air of contentment about him. A wave of embarrassment swept her—it'd been months, and beyond some Skype calls, she hadn't been able to meet the woman who'd helped him find that sense of peace.

"Clearly," she retorted. She moved to give him one of the quick squeezes that characterized the minimal physical affection they'd shared as adults. From him it was even more cursory than normal, barely a pat between her shoulder blades.

Pretending that didn't hurt like hell, she scrambled back and made brief eye contact with Ryan. He studied her with a blank, police-officer stare. Heat spread up her neck. He didn't get to pass judgment on her relationship with her family. Even if he seemed more comfortable in Maggie's kitchen than she did.

Years ago, her half siblings had, at her request, deleted the name *Ryan* from all their conversations. But she'd gleaned enough from offhand comments to know that Lachlan had maintained a friendship of sorts with her ex. And with what Maggie had just told Stella about feeling torn between the past and present, it made a bit more sense that he'd feel free to waltz into the house like all was well.

Needing something to do with her hands, she poured the men coffees, stirred in milk and passed them over.

Lachlan took it with a nod and sat at the table,

mumbling something to Maggie. Ryan accepted the mug with a stiff smile.

"Lunch break?" she asked. Hopefully it would end soon—as much as she wanted time with her siblings, she didn't want to share that time with Ryan.

He was in uniform, as he'd been this morning. It still fit him like he'd been made to wear it. Her breath hitched.

Which he noticed, damn it. Eyes glinting, he nodded. "Yep. Gave Lachlan a ride home from training." He slapped a palm to his forehead. "I forgot the supplies that the department gathered for your work bee. Want me to bring them tomorrow, or after work tonight?"

"Tonight." Lachlan gripped his coffee mug. "Bring it to my house. That way we can figure out what we still need for equipment."

"Aren't we having family dinner?" Stella asked. She'd assumed that would be the case, anyway. Though maybe she was persona non grata to the extent they didn't want to bother making a fuss…? An unfamiliar ache she didn't care to analyze squeezed her throat.

"Yeah, we were going to do something," Lachlan said grumpily. "Of course, that was before you decided to stay at a fricking hotel."

"Right." Her cheeks warmed. She peeked at Ryan out of the corner of her eye.

He was leaning against the counter, jaw locked

tight. "I'll drop off the stuff and be gone so fast, you won't even know I've been by."

And have everyone think she was clinging to the past by wanting to avoid him? No way. "Why don't you join us?"

Silence fell, the only sound the burbling coffee maker. Maggie and Lachlan froze, and Ryan was studying his boots. *Wow. Well done, self.* Hard to make it *more* uncomfortable, considering how pissed off Lachlan still was with her, but she'd managed to do just that.

"Probably better not to," Ryan said. "But thanks."

She couldn't decide whether to be relieved or annoyed by him declining the invitation. But much like that odd tightness in her throat, it was time to focus on something else. "Okay, then, our work bee—what still needs to be organized? We can make a list—"

"*Our* work bee?" Lachlan challenged.

"Yes, *our*," she said testily. He and Maggie seemed to be on the same wavelength about her use of *our*. Unsurprising. They always had shared a bond she hadn't been part of. She perched on the chair across from him and glanced at Ryan, who still looked in no hurry to leave. He made a "not my business, princess" face and took a drink of coffee.

"We have a list," Lachlan growled, clearly intent on making his point.

"Okay, but—" Stella cut herself off. "When is Gramps taking lunch?"

"He's not. He had an urgent care patient show up.

His shift ends at two thirty. But why you're so desperate to see him now but not for the last two months he's been in town—"

"Give her a break, Reid," Ryan commanded, quiet but sharp.

Stella froze at the order. She stared at Ryan. "I don't need you to fight my battles. And Lachlan's right to be mad at me."

"Is he, though?" Ryan's blue eyes filled with worry for a fraction of a second before he flattened his expression. "Maybe you deserve the benefit of the doubt."

She hid her shaking hands in her lap so he couldn't see them. Was he honestly defending her, or was he making some audacious, read-between-the-lines claim that *she* should be giving *him* the benefit of the doubt?

She looked pointedly at Ryan. "Could you leave us so we can hash this out?"

He straightened and put his half-finished coffee in the sink. "Gotcha. Good luck with that. I'll let myself out. See you all this evening."

The satisfaction she expected to feel at him leaving the room didn't come. Something about his tall frame, calmly leaning against the counter, had imbued the room with a sense of solidity, reliability.

As if Ryan can be relied on.

Maggie poked Lachlan with a finger. "Say what you need to say to get good with each other. Please. I don't want to be dealing with the two of you if you're mad all weekend."

"I'm not mad—" Stella stopped herself from finishing the excuse. Blaming Lachlan for being angry with her wasn't going to help.

"*I* am," Lachlan snarled. "Laura and Marisol are the best things that have ever happened to me, and you've barely bothered to try to get to know them, which is not surprising, since you've only been able to talk on Skype."

Stella stared at the table. "I know." She took in her brother's tight shoulders. "I would have been here earlier. Really. But my work project—it wasn't something I could leave."

"What kind of work project doesn't allow for a weekend off in four months?"

Her throat thickened. "One where your career is in jeopardy," she said honestly.

Maggie put down her sandwich, and Lachlan's mug landed on the table with a clunk. When coffee slopped over the side, he grabbed a napkin from the holder and dabbed at the mess. "What happened to your promotion?"

"It didn't turn out to be the advantage I'd hoped it would be." Her eyes filled with tears, and a half a year's worth of unspent tension built in her chest. She'd realized early on that her promotion wasn't going to be the boon she'd expected, but other than the investigators, she'd had no one to talk to since she'd made that call. Tears slid down her cheeks. She propped her elbows on the table and pressed the heels of her hands against her eyelids.

"Stella… Did you get fired or something?" Maggie asked.

Damn it. She'd said too much. She dropped her hands back into her lap and lifted her shoulders.

Lachlan reached over and rubbed a soothing circle on her back. "I'm sorry, Stella."

She shot him a half smile, and nodded at her sister. "Don't worry about the money I've put into the business. It won't be a problem."

The sooner the CIO and his cronies got charged, the better. They'd been lying to clients, using new investments to pay off old returns. If convicted, they faced either fines or jail time. Stella would potentially get a payout from the SEC's whistleblower fund, and depending on whether the accused parties got to stay on at the firm, anything from a hero's welcome to a pink slip. Technically, she wasn't supposed to get fired for whistleblowing. But her coworkers weren't particularly thrilled by her honesty and weren't going to make her life easy. They were worried about the health of the firm, about their own jobs. Some of them were wondering what else she knew, if they'd get named next. Or they thought she was in on it and covering her ass. However, they didn't know the whole story. She was holding out hope that once they learned the facts, they'd see why she did what she did. And maybe one day, she'd be able to explain it to Maggie and Lachlan, too.

Lach grimaced and leaned back in his chair. "You could have told us you were struggling."

Her nose stung. "No, I couldn't."

"Nice level of trust there, Stella," he retorted, tone short. "We're still business partners. And you don't think this could impact the business?"

"Seriously." Her tears broke free, choking her. "I-I c-couldn't."

An awkward silence fell around the table as Stella tried to suppress her tears and her siblings stared at her, both looking uncertain.

"I don't see why," Lachlan said, shifting his chair around so that he could wrap her in a strong hug. "But I haven't seen you cry since you were a teenager. I'm going to trust that you have a reason, and that one day you'll trust me enough to fill me in on why you're being so damn vague."

Her chest ached from crying and from the guilt of not being able to make it clear to her brother that her dishonesty had nothing to do with him. "Th-thank you."

"Well," he said, "you're still our partner, no matter what's happening in New York. You bailed me out after I got in too tight with Dad. I owe you for that."

"I'll be able to keep financing your business." She pulled away from his embrace and wiped her eyes.

Maggie and Lachlan shared an exasperated look. God, they'd been doing that since they were kids and it drove Stella nuts. Nothing like silent communication to remind a person that they were perpetually on the outside.

"Stop it with the money talk," Maggie said. "We didn't want you to come home for the money. It's about spending time with *you*. But not the finance-world you."

Stella swallowed. Easy for her sister to say. If Stella stripped away the identity she got from her job, what was left? And Sutter Creek was definitely not the place to find out what was buried under her years and years of all work, no play.

Chapter Six

Stella spent a few more hours at Maggie's place, going over renovation plans and finally seeing her grandfather, who was as fit and vivacious as ever. His quiet hug soothed a few of her still-jagged nerves. Her admission that her job was on the line seemed to have earned enough forgiveness that her brother was no longer snapping at her. But she wasn't so naive to believe that one teary apology would mend all the harm she'd caused.

She gave Lach a ride home, well aware that if her first time meeting Marisol in person didn't go well, any progress she'd made with her brother would be erased.

Her heart was in her throat by the time she parked

her rental in front of Lachlan's house. The olive-green split-level sat nestled by a small treed ravine on a quiet block close to the center of town. It was too weird that Lachlan and Marisol were living in Ryan's gran's old place. How many times had she sat on that front stoop with her ex, watching him throw a ball across the lawn for his gran's Westie? Or the times they'd sneaked around from the rear entrance and he'd jumped in the driver's seat of her falling-apart Tercel, and they'd just driven, hours of holding hands and laughing, with moments of silent comfort, too. He'd needed that, after his dad died. And she'd tried to be a refuge for him. Maybe that had been part of the reason why his desertion had cut such a ragged hole—when she'd been the one to need a shoulder to cry on, he hadn't reciprocated.

She shook her head. Time to create new memories to erase the old, to think of her brother and his family enjoying this space.

"Marisol knows we're coming?" she asked her brother, who was in the passenger seat, finishing up a reply to a supplier email that he'd gotten right before leaving Maggie's.

"Huh? Oh, yeah. I mean, she was ready last night."

"I wasn't," she said quietly.

He made a face. "Yeah. And I'm trying to understand why."

"My explanation of what's going on at work didn't make sense?"

"It explained why you couldn't come home." He

looked down at his fists, clenched in his lap. "Doesn't account for why you aren't staying with me or Maggie."

He wanted honesty? Okay. She could do that.

Sort of.

She swallowed, trying to calm her rising pulse. "Exhaustion. Being pissed at Ryan Rafferty for ticketing me. You living in Gertie's old house. Wanting to avoid a fight…" Her throat tightened. "How was I supposed to make a good impression when I was a stressed-out wreck and you were clearly furious with me?"

He rubbed his beard. Silence stretched between them. After what felt like minutes, he squeezed her shoulder. "You still feeling that way? A wreck?"

"I'll be fine." She could escape to the hotel room if dinner got to be too much. She motioned at the house. "Did the place come furnished, or did Gertie leave her furniture?"

"What, you worried she left behind the couch you lost your virginity on or something?" Lachlan climbed out of the car and shut the door.

She followed, slamming her own door harder than intended. "I didn't lose my virginity on a couch!"

Lachlan smirked. "In the barn, then."

Following him up the path bisecting the lawn, she swatted his arm. "Classified information."

"Better work on your poker face before tomorrow. You'll be at the scene of the crime, helping clean up. Though the loft is gone."

She frowned. "Not exactly something to be happy about, given the fire."

"It was already gone—contractor ripped it out during the original renos."

The front door opened. A curly-haired woman held the knob in one hand and a baby wrapped in a blanket against her shoulder with the other. Winter clothes covered her curvy figure. The reserved smile that she bestowed on Stella widened when she saw Lachlan.

"Hey, handsome, you're early. I haven't even thought about ordering dinner yet."

"All good—Gramps and Maggie and her crew aren't coming for another hour yet. But I was excited to come home to my girls." Lachlan jogged up the half flight of stairs. He kissed Marisol, then the top of the baby's head. A liver-brown-flecked dog shot past them and bounded down the stairs, nearly knocking Stella over and turning circles around her, covering her in little white dog hairs in three seconds flat. She'd forgotten how efficient pointers were at shedding on things—white hairs for dark clothes, and brown hairs for light.

"Not quite the body I hoped to greet first," Stella said, scratching the dog behind her soft brown ears, "but you're cute, too."

"Fudge!" Lachlan reprimanded. The dog immediately plopped its butt on the ground and cocked its head at Stella.

"Sure, now you remember your manners." She

brushed her hands down her coat. "Got a lint roller?" she asked her brother and Marisol.

They both chuckled.

At least the dog's greeting broke the ice a little.

"So nice to finally meet you in person," Marisol said to Stella before giving Lachlan a playful nudge. "How sweaty did you get while you were training? You need a shower."

He plucked the baby from Marisol's arm. "Laura doesn't mind, do you, nugget? Let's go inside so you can meet your auntie Stella." He disappeared into the house.

Stella climbed to the top of the stoop. Marisol kept holding the door, an inscrutable expression on her face. Her hesitance made sense—Marisol was firmly in Lachlan's corner, as she should be. Stella had kept herself out of the inner circle.

Marisol waited until Stella was inside with the door shut before she gave her a quick hug, her expression shifting to a stiff welcome. "You smell much nicer than your brother." She winced. "Sorry. That was weird. I'm punch-drunk from staring at textbooks all day. And we got all of two hours sleep last night… We're ordering takeout for dinner. Our fridge looks like it belongs to two people who have been cramming in work between caring for a cranky baby. My dad would be horrified I don't have any food suitable for company in the freezer, but we blew through his stock of potato dumplings months ago. The empanadas, too."

Stella was glad Marisol had belted out the barrage of rambling thoughts—it gave her a chance to look at the woman her half brother had decided to marry. They'd talked over video chats, so Stella was familiar with Marisol's green eyes and light brown skin, but meeting a person face-to-face got across the nuances lost on a screen. Something about Marisol, maybe her energy or posture, drew a person in. Similar to Lachlan, really. Probably why they'd found each other—like attracted like.

Probably why she and Ryan hadn't lasted. They'd been too different from each other.

Though he seems pretty driven these days. And I'm the one being dogged by a shady reputation.

Ugh, best she not dwell on any of that. She wouldn't succeed in winning her future sister-in-law's loyalty if she was distracted by relationship regrets the whole evening. "I'm the last person to point fingers about takeout. I live on it back home. Especially the last few months."

"Work troubles?" Marisol asked, waving Stella to the top floor of the split-level house.

"You could say that."

"I suspected there was something going on. Was it a problem worth breaking your brother's heart over?"

The words landed with a wallop, as Stella was sure they were intended to do.

"Ouch, Mari," Lachlan said, blowing raspberries on Laura's cheeks at the top of the stairs.

"I'll own that," Stella said. "And it was unavoidable."

Marisol made a face that Stella could only interpret as "I'll be the judge of that."

"We've started mending fences," Lachlan assured his fiancée. He passed the baby to Stella. "Here, have a baby. I'm told I need a shower."

She gingerly accepted the warm little bundle, and he jogged down the hall, leaving her to find her equilibrium holding Laura. She rested the baby's head in the crook of her elbow, snuggling the little body to her torso, so they could study each other's faces. And what a sweet face Laura had. A teeny, upturned nose and bow of a mouth, framed by a head full of dark, downy curls.

"Don't hold babies often?" Marisol asked, mouth twitching.

Stella jiggled her niece. She stared into the baby's hazel eyes. She and Ryan both had blue eyes. Their own baby probably would have—

She shook the thought from her head and smiled at her niece. "Honestly can't remember the last time I did," she admitted. "Not many of my friends back home have kids, and the few who do keep their work lives pretty separate from their families."

She waited, expecting a challenging comment from Marisol.

But the other woman nodded. "I find that at work, too."

"Yeah?"

"It's academia. Probably similar to your field when it comes to expectations for work-life balance. I've had to be clear about my boundaries since Laura was born."

"Boundaries at work. Ha," Stella said lightly, glancing around the room. Baby paraphernalia and outdoor equipment and psychology-themed texts covered every flat surface. The shag carpet of her youth was long gone, but she could still feel what it had been like to snuggle on the floor with Ryan, watching cheesy horror movies...

"You should try some," Marisol told her.

Some snuggles on the floor? Sure, but...no. That had been in her head, not part of whatever Marisol was talking about. "Huh?"

"Boundaries. They're good for you. Both in having enough at the office, but letting down your guard at home."

Stella blinked at her brother's fiancée. She sure didn't hold back. "Point taken."

"I hope so."

Good thing *point taken* and *point followed* were two different things. Stella was planning on working at mending the hurt she'd caused, but letting down her guard entirely felt like a stretch.

Hours later, around the dinner table, the closeness between Maggie and Lachlan and their partners drove home her inability to open up. She picked at the Thai takeout Maggie had brought, trying to participate in the conversation as her family recounted their days and spoke over each other. The mark of a group used to dining together. Even Asher and Ruth, who seemed lovely and kind, were more relaxed than Stella despite being new to the group.

So, relax.

That sounded like either Marisol or Maggie had infiltrated her conscience. Neither was welcome, not with useless advice like that.

She took another bite of her green curry and listened to her grandfather's rundown of the surgery he'd done over his lunch hour. Thankfully, beyond yet again twisting the truth about her quick exit from New York for Asher and Marisol's benefit, Stella hadn't been expected to share much.

She could handle people, but within the framework of numbers and investments. Without that structure, she was being asked to be emotionally naked, and she hadn't allowed herself to be that way in eons.

Close to the last time I sat in this room, in fact.

Except that time, she'd been picking at her dinner, trying to hide her queasiness from both Ryan and Gertie.

At least her indigestion tonight was solidly nerves, not pregnancy-related. Though cuddling Laura earlier… She could see why Marisol was happy to make room for parenthood and academia in her life.

Laura was in the living room on the floor with Ruth, who'd wolfed down her dinner for the chance to play with the baby.

The combination of baby giggles, little-girl laughs and Gramps's chuckle made Stella's heart pang. Lachlan and Marisol's fingers were casually linked on the table; they were eating one-handed. And Maggie only had eyes for her librarian. Not hard, given how handsome Asher was, with dark eyes and thick, near-black hair and one of the best pairs of glasses Stella had seen on a guy in ages. The navy plastic coordinated with his checked shirt. The orange paisley lining of his upturned cuffs had been catching her eye all evening, because he'd had his arm around Maggie for the majority of the meal.

Stella shook her head. "The domestic contentment going on here is hitting saccharine levels."

"You should try it," Maggie said. She smiled one of those insider-trading couple smiles at Asher.

Stella wasn't built for that kind of relationship. "Haven't managed to overcome the roadblocks with anyone."

"Like a business fire? Or unexpected parenthood? Anyone can overcome roadblocks, Stella. With some work," Lachlan said. He squeezed Marisol's hand, then glanced over at Laura, who was showing off her newly acquired rolling-over skills for Ruth.

Stella bristled. "I've done nothing *but* work since the moment I escaped this place."

Both her siblings stilled. Marisol glanced down, chewing her lower lip. Asher rubbed Maggie's back in a slow circle.

Gramps cleared his throat. "Not the kind of work that matters if you're wanting romance, honey."

She pressed her lips together, fighting the urge to retort that people looking for romance were asking to have their hopes dashed. She didn't want to rain on Maggie and Lachlan's lovey-dovey parades, nor did she have a hope of winning an argument about relationship longevity with Gramps, who'd kept a marriage alive for almost fifty years.

Hell, with the way her family members had handled the fire and Maggie's injuries, they'd probably be persevering with a fraud investigation at work, too. It was only Stella who wasn't holding it together. She was supposed to be the oldest, the role model, setting goals and achieving them. What was missing? Why were her siblings landing on their feet and she wasn't?

They have support.

Nah. It couldn't be so simple as lacking someone in her corner.

"I need to concentrate on fixing my messes, not on romance," she said to her grandfather.

"Seems one of your messes involves a past love," Gramps replied mildly.

"Has your breakup come up at all?" Lachlan asked.

Stella rested her chopsticks on her plate. "The sheriff was too busy giving me a ticket for us to get into the nitty-gritty about our history."

"You saw him again this morning, though," her brother pressed.

"And? Would you like me to text you every time I run into him?" She polished off her glass of wine and poured herself another, then took a long sip. "Don't forget that you brought him over to Maggie's today. Though at least you were present for that—you heard everything we said."

"You need to come clean," Lachlan said.

She felt the blood drain from her cheeks. The only thing she wanted to discuss less than her work troubles was her miscarriage. "Excuse me. I'm going to start cleaning up."

She jolted to her feet, grabbed her wineglass and plate and hurried into the kitchen.

Lachlan followed her, with Marisol close on his heels.

"There's nothing to clean up, Stell. What's the real problem?"

"'You need to come clean?' Not exactly dinner table conversation."

He shrugged. "You said you wanted to deal with your messes. And the fact Ryan doesn't know about your miscarriage is a pretty big mess."

Marisol drew in a sharp breath and covered her mouth with a hand.

A male throat cleared from behind Lachlan. "Seems I'm interrupting something confidential," their grandfather said, holding a squalling Laura out to Marisol. "Someone wanted her mama." He fixed a sorrowful look on Stella.

Heat blazed on her cheeks. "Gramps, I..." Not even knowing where to begin, she tossed back the rest of her wine and glared at her brother. "It's not confidential anymore."

"Lachlan," Marisol scolded, settling the baby against her chest. "That's really the kind of thing you should get permission to share."

Being the center of attention reminded Stella of the time she'd stepped on an ant nest as a kid—burning needles on her skin. The urge rose to grab her coat and purse and drive straight to the airport.

No. Face this head-on.

"Ryan was the one who cut off all contact, Lach," she stated quietly. "And sharing my personal business without explaining the context is a crappy thing to do."

"Sorry," Lachlan said. "I'm so used to Mari being family that I forgot you might not consider her part of your inner circle."

"Gramps didn't know, either," she reminded her brother. She shifted her gaze to her grandfather, who wore his typical expression of thoughtful compassion. "I'm sorry."

"No need to apologize for biology, honey," Gramps said, shuffling farther into the kitchen. He gave Stella a firm hug.

Wow. She'd gone from no comforting hugs for months to many in one day.

I could get used to this.

"Some of what went on the summer you graduated makes a bunch more sense, now," Gramps continued.

Lachlan looked at his fiancée, who shot him a warning look. When he turned back to Stella, his expression screamed "brace yourself to be psychoanalyzed." "It's not something you need to be ashamed of or anything."

"Stop making assumptions. I'm not ashamed." *But it still hurts. And it's been way too long for it to still hurt.* The backs of her eyes stung. She rubbed them with her fingertips. "I'm sorry, Marisol. You're getting a *great* first impression of me. Me not telling Ryan—it's a long story."

Marisol tilted her head, her expression soft. "My ex-husband walked out on me right after I had a second-trimester miscarriage. I'm the last person who would judge, or assume a person's safe to tell another about something so intimate."

Oof, there was more than one thing to process there. "It's not a safety issue with Ryan, I promise."

Lachlan's eyes snapped with an unspoken challenge: *then what is it?*

She met her brother's questioning gaze. "I've always figured it's better to leave the past in the past. We've both moved on."

"At the risk of sticking my nose in where it doesn't belong," Marisol said, jiggling the baby in her one-armed embrace, "that's not always realistic. Because if you're hurting, the past *isn't* in the past. It's affecting your present."

Stella couldn't deny that, so she nodded. But running off to Ryan and applying said advice wasn't the way to go. Dredging up their history would only cause more pain. Better to live with the hurt she knew rather than create new ones.

"That's a good point," she conceded, not wanting to alienate Marisol, who was clearly just trying to help. But being the focus of the conversation was not working, not while her eyes were threatening to leak and she couldn't force a smile. "Excuse me for a sec."

A quick trip to the bathroom wasn't going to cut it. She escaped out the front door.

She sat on one of the middle steps. The cold from the concrete stairs seeped through the seat of her jeans and the soles of her thick socks. Right. She'd left her boots inside. And her cashmere sweater was cozy, but not when facing the January chill.

At least she was alone, though. She buried her face in her palms and tried to breathe away the threat of tears. Damn it. It was as if when she'd crossed the state line, her eyes became determined to prove her wrong about never crying.

The roar of a truck engine approached and stopped nearby. Measured boot steps rang in her ears, coming up the path. She dropped her hands from her face, stiffening when she recognized the visitor. "Ryan. Hey. I forgot you were planning to come by."

It was the first time since she arrived that she'd

seen him in civilian's garb. Jeans, winter boots and a thick, plaid jacket. A thin beanie covered his dark hair. He filled out his casual clothes even better than he had his uniform. An athlete would covet those thighs and shoulders. No doubt he'd be able to beat a suspect in a foot race. And with all he'd bulked up, his hoodies would be even bigger and cozier than the one she'd habitually stolen in high school.

He eased onto the step next to her. "You okay, Stella? You look upset."

The stair was wide, but not wide enough to fit both of them and their emotional baggage. She inched away from him and crossed her arms. "I'm fine."

"I'd offer you my jacket, but I figure you'd burn it before accepting it from me," he said.

"I wouldn't go that far," she muttered.

"We ready to relax around each other yet?"

"Even if I was, dinner with my family is the opposite of relaxing."

"Oh?" he said. "Entertaining meal? Is that why you're out in the cold?"

Her pulse picked up. As if she'd admit that they'd been talking about him. "Needed fresh air."

He glanced up at the sky. "Going to get some snow, too, if you wait a few more minutes. As well as a frozen ass. Probably better you face whatever drove you outside rather than hiding on the front stoop in your socks."

She let out a grumble. Restraint, really, when she

wanted to tell him to piss off. Or worse. "Thanks for the pro tip."

"What is it you're avoiding?" He stretched his legs out in front of him and rested his elbows on one of the stairs behind him.

"Make yourself comfortable, why don't you," she snapped.

He shook his head. "You're so damn prickly. And I know that's partly to do with our past, but I'd hoped we could move on."

"Not everything is about you," she said, way shriller than she'd have liked.

"Family didn't accept your apology for staying away for so long?" he speculated.

"They were fine!" The damn tears she'd been trying to fight managed to slip out.

He slowly straightened, his posture now alert. "There's a *but* there, Stella." He shucked off his jacket and draped it over her shoulders. It was lined with faux-shearling fleece, and smelled delicious. Like sunny days and a hint of citrus. Not his high-school, department-store-cologne scent. But it was something new she wouldn't mind learning. Jolting at the realization, she mumbled a thank-you and gripped the sides tight in front of her. The intimacy inherent in wearing his coat made her stomach wobble. But without the warmth and his silent support, she might dissolve even worse.

He wiped the tears away from her cheeks with his thumbs. His skin was even warmer than the jacket lining, leaving a trail of heat along her chilly face. Some misguided, lonely part of her came to life, urging her to scoot closer. The rest of him would be toasty and solid, too, which sounded—

Wrong. It sounds wrong.

She shifted away from him a few more inches.

He frowned, and dropped his hand. "It takes guts, coming back here and trying to make amends."

Guts. Ha. If she was actually brave, she'd take Lachlan's advice and come clean. Tell Ryan why it had been so devastating when he'd turned her away, which had been compounded by the loss soon after. That pain had only faded, never disappeared. And being in Sutter Creek meant that loss was coming back into focus, regaining some of the sharp edges that had softened over time.

"It's hard right now, but give it time. You'll be glad you came home." He squeezed her knee before walking back to his truck. "Get some shoes on and come help me unload this stuff."

She settled a shaking hand on her leg, which tingled with the echo of his touch. Damn it.

But she did as he suggested, retrieving her boots and running a couple of loads of construction supplies into Lachlan's basement. After, she and Ryan both entered the main floor. Her grandfather was holding the baby and chatting with Marisol in the living room. Ruth and Asher were clearing the table. Everyone greeted Ryan with friendly grins or hellos, except for her grandfather, whose mouth firmed in a hard line.

"Problem, Gramps?" she asked.

He shook his head quickly, as if trying to clear it. "It's been a while since I saw the two of you enter a room together."

"Nothing to see here," Stella said. "Ryan was just dropping off the donations for the work bee." She went into the kitchen. Ryan followed. "Sorry I left for so long," she said to Lachlan and Maggie, who were loading the dishwasher and murmuring about something. "I was getting too warm. All that spicy food."

Doubt crossed Lachlan's face. And Maggie's expression turned downright incredulous.

"What?" Stella said.

"Nice jacket," her sister said, mouth twitching.

She whipped off the garment and shoved it at Ryan before grabbing the wineglass on which Marisol had written *Stella* in gold pen. She poured herself another glass and drank a third of it. "I got cold."

Maggie and Lachlan traded knowing smiles.

"But you were too hot," her sister pointed out. "All that spicy food."

"It was hot in here. Not out there," she said, taking another sip. "It's been a long day. I think I'll head back to the hotel."

"How many glasses of wine have you had?" Ryan asked.

"Two plus this," she said before wincing. "Shoot, I wasn't thinking. I barely drive my car in

Manhattan—I'm not used to counting at dinner."
And she really wanted to get out of here before everyone started in on the questions about what she
and Ryan had been discussing outside.

"Need a chauffeur?" he offered.

Stella glanced at him. He looked genuine in his
offer—unless he wanted to use the time to prod her
about her feelings some more. And Lach and Maggie looked exceedingly interested by the invitation.
What was better, sibling interrogation about borrowing his coat now, or about accepting a ride later?

Definitely later.

"Yeah, I'll take you up on that," she told Ryan.

He was waiting in the truck by the time she retrieved her coat and said her goodbyes. She climbed in.

Stella put on her seat belt, tension squeezing her
shoulders and neck. *We ready to relax around each
other yet?* he'd asked earlier.

Easy answer to that one. *Nope.*

He'd draped the jacket she'd borrowed across
the console. The truck was by no means tidy, but
it wasn't a pigsty, either. Just lived-in, with a few
things scattered in the back seat—a dog leash,
snowboarding boots, a gym bag. Aside from the
sheriff's-department sticker on the back window,
the late-model Ford wasn't recognizable as belonging to law enforcement.

"Where's all your cop gear?" she asked. "Thought
you drove a county vehicle."

"Not usually when I'm off shift," he explained,

steering them out of the neighborhood. "So tell me more about living in Manhattan."

"Well, it's cold, but in a different way," she said, trying to snuggle farther into her coat.

With one hand, he picked his jacket off the console and draped it haphazardly across her torso. The scent of his jacket, masculine and comforting, curled into her nostrils.

Okay, seriously. He collected supplies for the barn bee, played taxi and was dedicated to his job—no wonder why people elected him. It was way too easy to ignore his past sins with so much evidence he was a beyond-decent person. Why couldn't he act like the jerk she'd cast him as for so long?

Except those sins affected me more than they did the town.

Which meant that maybe Lachlan was right. Maybe opening up about her miscarriage could make it possible to finally find closure. She didn't need Ryan's friendship back. But if honesty let her live a little easier herself, and removed a barrier preventing her from feeling comfortable in the town where her half siblings lived…? Might be worth it.

Her heart thunked like a bass drum.

"Ryan?" Her voice cracked.

"Yeah?"

"I have something to tell you."

Ryan focused on the road, gripping the steering wheel hard enough to feel the leather compress.

Good grief. Things just couldn't be simple today. People wanting something from him—talk about a theme.

And it went beyond his prodigal ex-girlfriend. His campaign supporters wanted him to be devoted to the county. His grandmother wanted him to be cautious around Stella.

So what did *he* want?

For starters, he didn't want Stella to break her NDA on his behalf. And her expression and quick breaths suggested an imminent confession.

He rubbed his jaw, the rasp of his five o'clock shadow rough against his palm. "I think whatever you have to say is best left unsaid."

She turned toward him, eyes narrowed. "How do you know?"

"Just a hunch," he stated. He couldn't let her break the law. Nor could he afford to get closer to her. "I get that now that you've jumped on the 'spill your guts' train, you're wanting to make the ride worth it. But we don't have to churn up a whole lot of things you don't really want to talk about."

She blinked in surprise. "What happened to facing the things I was avoiding?"

You looking at me like I'm both the reason for and answer to your problems.

"It was the right thing to do with your family," he said instead.

"But not with you?" she asked.

Drawing to a halt at a stop sign, he used the pause

to take a long look at Stella, her blue eyes wide and plump lips pursed in question. Her analytical mind was clearly clicking away, like always. And she looked too damn good with his coat tucked up under her chin like a blanket.

"No, not with me."

She released a long breath and settled into the seat. The wrinkle between her eyebrows softened.

Maybe she hadn't wanted to open up any more than he'd wanted to be on the listening end.

He accelerated, driving on the road that looped toward the chateau-style hotel. Once upon a time, he and his high-school buddy Rafe had drag-raced along this road. Now, he ticketed people for doing the same. Or for driving too fast for conditions…

"I'm sorry I had to ticket you last night," he said.

She snorted. "Sure."

"I'm the one who brought in the extra diligence policy after that fatality. If I got a reputation for playing favorites…"

"Pretty sure everyone understands that's not the case with me," she muttered.

He wasn't sure that was what the townsfolk believed at all. Nor was he certain they were wrong in that assessment.

He and Stella might have been completely wrong for each other, mainly in that she had deserved a person with a full range of emotions. Back then, his had topped out somewhere between stunted and stifled. But he still favored her, a hell of a lot.

Enough that it probably hadn't been smart to offer her a ride tonight.

"Can you drop me off behind that little grocery store off Main Street? I'll walk to the hotel from there."

"Uh, I guess." Another block and he pulled his truck into the parking lot. "The path to the lift base is well-lit." Sutter Creek was safe—he made sure of that—but like anywhere, it wasn't a great idea for a person to walk down dark alleys alone.

"If I can handle New York, I can handle Main Street at eight o'clock at night."

The dark circles under her eyes said she wasn't handling New York. Her job problems appeared to be taking a toll.

And unless you want to lose your own job, you need to keep that concern at a distance.

"Don't give me that 'them there streets are dangerous, little lady' look, Sheriff."

"I was thinking about you looking tired, not whether or not you're safe in whatever Tribeca enclave you've ensconced yourself in."

"Upper West Side," she grumbled, opening the truck door and slipping out. "And no need for you to concern yourself with either my sleep debt or my safety." She cleared her throat. "Thanks for the ride. Way better ending than the last time you tried to drive me home."

He cringed. "Do me a favor and don't bring that up too often in public."

People had forgiven him, but forgiveness was easily retracted.

She shivered, then nodded.

He tossed her his jacket off the seat. "If you're going to insist on walking, at least take an extra layer." He fully expected her to reject the offer, but she nodded again and slung the fabric overtop her sleek wool coat.

"It'll mean we'll have to meet up again," she cautioned him.

"You know where to find me," he replied, draping an arm across the back of the seat in an attempt to look casual.

"But I don't particularly want to." She turned on a heel and headed for the back entrance to the grocery store.

He stared at her retreating form. She might not want to see him again, but they were going to have to spend time together at the work bee. He'd have to make sure they were working in different areas, because the thought of Stella wielding power tools was enough to make him lose concentration and chop off a finger with a drywall saw. And the last thing he needed was to have one of his friends come at him with an "is that a hammer in your pants, or are you just happy to see Stella?" gibe.

Surely with all the work to do, it wouldn't be hard to keep her at a safe distance.

Chapter Seven

Gran's text came in early Saturday morning as Ryan was getting ready to go help out at the Reids's barn.

What's the name of the company where Stella works?

He drained the rest of his coffee and shot off a reply. Holden Management. Why?

CNN is reporting something about investigation rumors.

Anxiety panged in his stomach. If Stella's name got dragged into this, her life was about to get a whole lot worse.

Before he could respond, another message arrived. *If she's up to no good, and it's known you're chatting her up over coffee and ferrying her all over hell's half acre, you're going to get questions.*

He shook his head. The only thing he was going to get was indigestion caused by grandmotherly interference.

Let me see what I can find out.

He had twenty minutes before he needed to leave, so he poured himself another coffee, booted up his laptop and did some cursory searching. There wasn't much to be found in regard to the rumors Gran had mentioned, or speculation on what it could mean. Stella wasn't talked about anywhere. And if she was working with federal investigators, with no plea agreement in place, it was unlikely there'd been criminal activity or an ethical breach on her part. But he didn't like the position she was in. The people at her company had a lot to lose, and if Stella took the brunt of that...

Not what Gran was worried about, so he could at least be honest with her.

I'm not seeing anything to be concerned about on the public record, he texted. Telling Gran that his stomach was twisting at the prospect of potential harm to Stella would be asking for a headache.

He was lacing up his work boots when his phone rang. He didn't need call display to tell him Gran had given up on text messaging. He put it on speaker so that he could keep getting ready. "Yes?"

"I'm not convinced, Ryan."

"You're going to have to be. I can't find anything else out without making some calls or digging into records, and that would be overreaching, nor could I disclose anything I found to you, anyway," he said, pulling a hoodie out of the hall closet.

"Humph. Maybe *I'll* do some poking around."

He froze with his sweatshirt half over his head. "No."

"Nothing obvious, honey, but if we're going to look out for your reputation—"

"Trust me to handle it." Pulling his hoodie on the rest of the way, he picked up his cell from the hall table and clicked it off speaker. "I have a building blitz to get to."

"Will Stella be there?"

"They're expecting a crowd, so I assume yes." *Hope so, more like it. All levels of stupid.* "And do me a favor—stop wasting your Saturday on CNN."

"We'll see," she said.

It wasn't the promise of noninvolvement he wanted, but he needed to hit the road.

A half hour later, he was already sweating, help-ing Lachlan haul in fresh sheets of drywall. The res-toration company had stripped away the damaged materials and the emergency contractor had shored up the sections that were weight-bearing, so now it was grunt-work time. Framing in the rooms, mounting drywall, replacing windows…

"You know," Asher Matsuda complained, working alongside Ryan and Lachlan, "I swear I already did this once."

Ryan snorted. "You'll be extra fast, then. Though I figured we wouldn't see you today, being Saturday." Asher was Jewish, and usually didn't work on Shabbat.

Asher shrugged and put his hands on his hips, scanning the interior with his experienced eye. "I'm not getting paid, it's a family affair and it's an off-week for our synagogue—we meet biweekly—so I'm calling in a technicality. Plus, Ruth had ski practice. I would have been at loose ends."

"Whatever gives us an extra set of hands," Lachlan said. "Rafe should be here soon, too. And Maggie and Stella are on a hardware-store run."

"Hadn't wondered," Ryan lied.

"BS," Lachlan said, muffling the callout with a cough.

Ryan shot him the finger and got back to work.

Between the Reid family, the clinic employees and a few of Lachlan's search-and-rescue crew who were there to pitch in, it was an efficient crowd. Ryan hammered, lifted and taped for an hour, eventually stripping down to his T-shirt. Soon after, his buddy Rafe arrived, and they traded insults and filled each other in on their weeks while working. Rafe owned the ranch next to Georgie Halloran's, and had been hit by the cattle theft ring, too. He was as anxious as Georgie that the culprits be discovered and arrested.

"Hello, busy bees!" Gran greeted from the doorway. Maggie and Stella followed her, each carrying a cardboard tray with travel cups. "I ran in to your shopping crew at the bakery and came along to deliver coffee!"

Deliver coffee, my ass. Keep an eye on Stella is more like it.

Stella pointedly didn't look at him, taking her tray to the opposite side of the large space to pass out drinks to the search-and-rescue crew.

All right then. They were pretending the other didn't exist. Exactly what he'd planned to do, especially with Gran in the building. So why did it chafe?

His grandmother did a piss-poor job of hiding her glances between him and Stella, clearly registering the purposeful distance. She took her travel tray to Maggie's receptionist and his husband, a physical therapist at the health center where Ryan went to the gym.

Maggie sauntered toward him and plucked a travel cup out of the cardboard tray she was balancing on her forearm, probably to avoid holding any weight with her bandaged hands. "We meet again, Sheriff."

"Didn't realize you were keeping track," Ryan said.

"I'm not." She waved a hand at their surroundings. "I meant in here."

He took the drink from her. "Gotcha. Can't say I

spend a lot of time thinking about that. Much more of a fan of walls that aren't on fire."

Or ceilings. Or construction detritus, burning two feet away from a passed-out Maggie. He suppressed a shudder.

She blanched. "Good point."

Gran bustled over and put a hand on Maggie's shoulder. "Maggie, honey, you look like you've seen a ghost."

"Yeah, mine," she murmured under her breath.

"You and Ryan were both brave that day." Gran patted Maggie's cheek. Maggie didn't seem to mind the mothering gesture. Gran raised her voice as she went around the room to give Lachlan, Rafe and Asher their coffees. "We ran into Georgie Halloran at the hardware store. She said to say hello and that she'll come help out tomorrow."

Stella's frown caught Ryan's eye. She stood next to her brother, wearing a pair of jeans that were way too fancy for construction work. Her sweatshirt, emblazoned with the Sutter County Search and Rescue insignia, must have been one of Maggie's. Or Lachlan's, maybe, given it was a little big on Stella. She hadn't yet made eye contact with Ryan, and her back was still stiff from his grandmother's announcement.

"That's kind of Georgie," Ryan said. Gran wore a wily, calculated expression that made the back of his neck prickle.

"She's bringing Emma," Gran continued, staring at him.

"Great. Though why you're directing that at me, I don't know. I'm just a worker bee."

"Georgie thought you should know," his grandmother said.

Ryan groaned inwardly. Apparently, the rancher hadn't believed him when he'd told her nothing was going to happen between him and her daughter.

Maggie snorted and raised an eyebrow at Gran. "More to the point, Georgie was wanting my opinion on Ryan's opinion on Emma. And Stella's opinion on—"

"Maggie," Stella snapped.

Shrugging, Maggie pitched the empty cardboard tray in a recycle bin and joined Asher over by the half-built wall that would become Lachlan's new office.

Ryan lifted his chin at Gran. "Feel free to mark out some measurements and cut boards if you're not heading back to the bakery."

"I can pitch in for an hour," she said, motioning for him to pass over the tape measure. "Let's mount some drywall."

"I bet the drywall also wants to know Maggie's opinion on your opinion of Emma Halloran, Sheriff," Lachlan called out, laughing.

"I can't speak for Maggie, but I know mine is that she's a good woman who has no interest being married to law enforcement." He pointed at Maggie. "And I'm betting you'd be breaking all sorts of best-friend laws if you colluded with Emma's mom in playing matchmaker."

"Collusion," Gran said. "Honestly, Ryan."

He chanced a glance at Stella. Her arms hung loose at her sides. Brow furrowing, she pulled her lower lip in between her teeth.

"Setting Emma up is in no way on my agenda," Maggie said. "But I don't see why you're so opposed. You guys would be cute together."

"You mentioned wanting a wife and family, dear," Gran added.

Stella gasped, loud enough that a half-dozen heads swiveled in her direction. Her face paled. Then she coughed, thumping a fist against her chest. "Sorry. Must have inhaled some dust."

It was a decently convincing act, but Ryan was trained to pick up on lies. And Stella Reid had just dropped one on her family and their employees.

She locked gazes with him. Those blue irises were a wallop to the gut. He kept his gaze on hers when he said, "You got me there, Gran. Pretty sure I've figured out my past crap enough that I'd make a decent husband and dad."

Now it was a matter of finding someone who believed it, too.

So, Ryan had figured out his past crap? *Must be nice.* Stella's hands shook, and she stuck them in the pockets of the hoodie she'd borrowed from her brother.

Why was she even affected by Ryan knowing what he wanted from life? She knew what she wanted—why should it be different for him? As if she gave a hoot whom he dated, or if he wanted to be a family man.

He almost was a dad. And doesn't even know.

She growled. Her conscience needed to lay off. For one, she had been barely pregnant when she miscarried. And two, she never would have kept it a secret had she carried to term. Like he said yesterday, there was no need to churn up things she didn't want to revisit. The past could stay in the past.

Though Gertie Rafferty didn't seem on board with that. She needed to stop sending not-so-subtle messages that Stella wasn't welcome here. The older woman had been downright antagonistic at the bakery when Maggie and Stella had put in their order for the crew.

It was time to make it clear that she wasn't intending on staying in town any longer than necessary. Crossing the room, she halted in front of Ryan and his gran, who were busy measuring sheets of drywall.

"Gertie, thanks for coming to help today," she greeted. "Before you're elbows-deep, let's catch up outside for a few minutes."

"What's there to catch up on?" Gertie asked. Her tone was neutral, but her eyes flashed with challenge.

"You seem a little misinformed about why I came home, and—"

"Oh, I know why you came home. It's all over the news."

Stella's cheeks went numb. She'd seen the rumor reports this morning, but she hadn't thought anyone would clue in so quickly. And her name hadn't been mentioned…

Be chill. "Not sure what you mean."

"Oh, lordy," Gertie muttered.

Ryan locked gazes with her, questioning, probing.

She looked away. Since when had he become so observant about her emotional state?

Give him some credit. Their relationship may have ended with silence and rejection, but before that, he'd cared for her feelings. He'd been mad at the world in high school, but never at her. So much so that she'd shared everything with him, in the loft of this barn, back when it still stretched the length of what was now the multipurpose area. They'd fumbled their way, finding pleasure, joy, surprise. Making foolish promises.

And when he'd told her he was ending it, and actually stuck to it, she'd made promises to herself. Mainly, in young, hyperbolic fashion, that she'd hate his guts forever.

Also foolish—obviously that was pointless. And, hell, maybe he'd been the brave one. Seeing reality, that they weren't suited.

Did he see through her now, too?

She shivered. This barn was too small for the both of them. "I wonder if there's anything outside that needs doing. The landscaping took a beating, could use some attention."

Ryan and Gertie both looked at her like she was off her rocker.

"Bit hard to landscape when the ground's frozen," Ryan said.

"I know," she retorted.

"You always knew best, didn't you?" Gertie said. "Leaving with barely a word. Hurting your family by staying away."

"Seriously?" Stella did not need snide comments from Gertie when it was *her* grandson who'd left first. "I think we need to clear up a few things."

"Incorrect," Gertie said, calmly drawing marks on a sheet of drywall.

Of all the stubborn—

Ryan's hand landed on Stella's shoulder. Strong and steady, on the surface. But he wasn't. Or at least he hadn't been when it mattered. Nor had she, for that matter—the reason Gertie's accusations pricked so deeply was the truth in them.

He leaned in close. "Just leave it for now, okay? I'll talk to her later."

Tearing herself away from his grip, from the temptation to lean into his reassuring strength, she snapped, "What, you get to speak your mind and I don't?"

"Let's not—" He jammed his hand into his hair and didn't continue.

Gertie narrowed her eyes. "What's there to ex-

plain? Your company's going under and you're involved in it, so you're trying to hide out here."

"What?" That's what Gertie had taken from the
brief speculation on the news today? Frustration tore
through Stella. What she'd give to be able to defend
herself. But she couldn't say a word.

Fine. If the older woman wanted to draw false
conclusions, might as well give her something
equally untrue to chew on.

Forcing a smile, she settled a hand on Ryan's biceps. Heat spread from her fingers to her arm, threatening to spill to her core. She breathed, ignoring the
tease of touching him. "I left your jacket in my rental.
I'll run out and get it."

The jaw-dropped dismay on Gertie's face was so
worth the cost of cupping that rock-hard biceps.

Was it really?

Okay, maybe not. Her hand was threatening to de-
velop a mind of its own and slide across to his chest
to test whether his pecs were as taut as his arm muscles. Squeezing a little tighter to resist the urge, she
smiled at Gertie. "Excuse me for a second."

She headed for the door. Heavy, booted footsteps
followed.

Cold air slapped her face as she opened the door
and tucked her hands inside her sleeves.

"Stella." Ryan caught her elbow. "What *was
that*?"

She shivered from his touch.

Okay, this was ridiculous. She'd survived in one

of the most high-pressure jobs on Wall Street. Why the hell was she shaky from having her former high-school boyfriend touch her arm?

She schooled her features and ignored the tempting pressure of his palm. "Pretty sure *that* was your grandmother and me competing for the petty crown. What did *you* think it was?"

Regret flickered in his eyes and he scrubbed a hand down his face. "If people get the wrong idea and it gets back to Georgie Halloran—"

"Why is she up in your business, anyway?" she interrupted, turning around the back corner of the veterinary clinic, the squat little house her grandfather had purchased and converted early in his career.

"She's one of my major campaign supporters, and needs me to be wholeheartedly devoted to Sutter County."

She shot him a look. "And me being in town affects that how?"

"You've been gone a while."

"Exactly. Long enough for people to forget we ever dated."

Shaking his head, he let out another disbelieving laugh. "It's been so long since anyone saw you, they have no frame of reference. They still connect you to me, because they don't have a new picture of who you are."

Which meant either being connected to Ryan in perpetuity, or letting people see who she was now. "I'm not sure I know who I am."

He paused, speaking cautiously after a few beats of silence. "What's that supposed to mean?"

She felt the blood drain from her cheeks. Oh, dear. She really hadn't meant to say that out loud. She rounded the front of the clinic and opened the hatch of her SUV with the key fob. Once the door lifted all the way, she leaned against the bumper, crossing her arms over her borrowed sweatshirt. The quiet side street was empty, as always. And right across the street was Maggie's yard. Snow covered the rhodos and flower beds, but it looked like her half sister had been keeping up with their grandparents' green-thumb ways since taking over the house. Not a gene Stella had inherited.

"Stella?" Ryan prodded, hitching a hip next to her. He had to duck to fit under the hatch, and the angle brought him close to her. In another life, she would have palmed his cheek and stolen a kiss.

Instead, she exhaled and pretended she had no interest in seeing if he still tasted like mint Tic Tacs. "I'm assuming your grandmother filled you in on what she saw on the news today?"

"Yes."

"I can't talk about it," she said.

He grimaced. "Then don't."

"Thank you," she murmured. Fussing with a hangnail on her thumb, she avoided his gaze. She could at least tell him what she'd told Maggie and Lachlan. It wasn't covered under her NDA. "I don't know if I have a job to go back to."

He made a face. "Based on what I heard on the news today, why do you want to go back to that?"

She carefully thought over how to phrase her answer. "Most of the people in my industry are ethical. Competitive, yes. But trustworthy. And I excel at my job. I fit in."

He lifted an eyebrow.

"What?"

"Can't be that good a fit if you needed to escape," he said gently.

"I didn't—" Ugh, enough of sounding defensive. "I'm on vacation. But lucky for you and your now-sterling reputation, I'm only staying a few weeks."

"Gran's convinced you're up to no good."

She grimaced. "And you think so, too."

"No, but for the sake of her staying off my back, could you not provoke her?"

"I'm not going to take her crap lying down, Ryan." She bristled, remembering Gertie's tone today. "She's being unfair. I wasn't even planning on contacting you during this visit—it's a fluke that we've seen each other so much. I'm supposed to be focusing on Lachlan and Marisol and their families, not you."

"Their families are *your* family, Stell." He settled a hand between her shoulder blades and rubbed a slow circle.

Stupid, being affectionate in a public place. But it felt too good to remind him.

"That remains to be seen. I don't know them well yet. But the thought of bonding with my half siblings is nice. The fire was a bit of a wake-up call. Except, I—"

Her thoughts whirled, and she stared at Ryan, let herself get sucked into his deep blue gaze for a second. Once upon a time, she'd confessed all her insecurities to him. Did he remember? Would he recognize the doubt on her face? She fisted her hands to stop from twisting her fingers together, an old, bad habit she'd broken when she realized making it in finance would mean hiding her feelings.

"I think they want to get closer, too," he said softly.

And if they didn't? She feigned nonchalance. "Is it really worth the effort with everyone? Once I'm gone, they'll forget about me all over again."

"They never forgot, Stella." He cleared his throat and brushed a thumb along her jaw. "Neither did I. Never have, never will."

His thumb traced perilously close to the corner of her mouth, and he leaned in. She hadn't forgotten *this*, that was for sure. Breath brushing across lips. Callused fingers drawing a lazy pattern—

"Wait, what are we doing?" She sprang back, whacking her head on the hatch in the process. "Ouch." She rubbed the aching spot.

"Not thinking, that's for sure." He rubbed his jaw. "Kinda wish you'd come to your senses about ten seconds later, though."

She grabbed his jacket from where it was draped over the back seat and shoved it at him, then put her hands on her hips. "You forgot about me easily enough when you turned me away from that ranch."

His eyes shuttered closed. "Crap, Stella, I'm so sorry..."

"You should be." In more ways than he knew. "Doesn't mean you were wrong about the end result, though. I'm not the small-town girl you need."

And if she gave in and kissed him, even for curiosity's sake, she'd be leaving Sutter Creek in more turmoil than when she arrived.

Chapter Eight

"I read that some huge ethics scandal is being covered up. She must have been involved if she's back here."

Gertie Rafferty's ears perked up at the conversation behind her. She slapped a rag on the bakery table she was wiping down, recognizing the chatty trio as contemporaries of Ryan's back in high school. Not that the group clustered at the wall-length bistro bar would have given him the time of day back then. His sulky, standoffish routine hadn't endeared him to the popular crowd, no matter how good-looking he'd been as a boy. He'd had to learn to glad-hand. Stella had been the one all the other kids had wanted to emulate. Not anymore, apparently. She was keeping the gossip fires burning today.

"And did you see the way she was looking at Sheriff Rafferty when they were in here a few days ago? I bet they're still hooking up."

"He'd know all about scandals."

The tittering laughs made the hair on the back of Gertie's neck rise, and she scrubbed the table harder. The nerve of them, coming into her family's bakery and churning up trouble.

"Ethics, too," the lone man in the group interjected. "Right up Rafferty's alley."

Oh, that was it.

"The white doesn't come off, you know." A smooth male voice interrupted her, just as she opened her mouth to pelt the group with a piece of her mind.

She turned and fixed Tom Reid with a scolding look. "They're cream, not white. And if I didn't scrub them, they'd turn beige in a week."

He chuckled. A short goatee framed his friendly smile. The man was as handsome at all get-out with his full head of white hair and military-grade posture. He'd been out on the ski hill enough since he came back to town that he'd kept his Arizona tan. Things she should not be noticing, given he was well and truly taken by a sixtysomething blond bombshell he'd met on the Arizona golf links. Far as Gertie knew, he'd be returning to his sunshine home as soon as Maggie could go back to work full-time.

"Your Nancy knows how to wipe a table," he said.

"I'm sure she and Viv would be fine without you hovering."

Her daughters were exceedingly competent; the bakery brought in a profit far higher than it had when Gertie had been at the helm. She might have fallen short when it came to raising her son, but Viv and Nancy proved she'd had some successes among her failures. As did Ryan. He was a heck of a credit to their family. Though he'd done most of that himself... Her throat pinched. She'd officially reached the point in her life where she was expendable. A rotten realization. And just because Tom had his new life down in Arizona didn't give him the right to poke fingers at hers. "When are you planning to fly south again?"

His lips turned down at the corners. "Maybe never."

"Oh?" Curiosity pulled at her.

He took a drink from his coffee cup and motioned at the seat across from him.

Giving the empty table a final wipe, she folded the rag and placed it on the corner of Tom's table before sitting in the proffered chair.

A peal of laughter erupted from the trio at the wall counter, and she crossed her arms and glared at them.

"Well now, Gertie, can't point fingers at that group for passing around news when you're eager to hear *my* latest."

"It's different." She clenched her hands, wishing she could give her short hair a pat to check for strays, but she didn't want to touch it after just holding a cleaning cloth. "I'm merely intrigued by the goings-on of a friend. They're being malicious—about your granddaughter as much as my Ryan, I'd point out. Throwing around words like *scandal* and *ethics*."

Stella had been in town for four days, and as much as her appearance was giving everyone something to chat about over their morning croissants, Tom's arrival two months ago had been discussed almost as much. Half of the members of Gertie's book club were pretending their tabbies and Pomeranians were ill. Any excuse to book an appointment with Dr. Tom.

"I'm hoping that things will turn around for said granddaughter," he said. "She can't talk about whatever is going on, apparently. But I'm worried."

Well, that did nothing to quell her curiosity, but she could respect the need for privacy. Given the piece she'd seen on CNN, more details would be made public soon.

"There was a vague news report," she confided. "And who knows with that generation. Facebook and Instagram and Snapchat and no sense of the damage that can be done. In our day, we at least had to talk about people to their faces." She grinned sheepishly.

Tom laughed.

Lordy, it felt good to make a man laugh.

Ridiculous, Gertie. She only had so much time in a day, and needed to focus on her family, not on Tom Reid's handsome grin.

She shook her head. "I thought she'd put Sutter Creek well and truly past her."

"As did I. But something's changed," he mused, taking a small bite of his pastry and swallowing. "Mmm, that's almost as good as when you made them." He shook his head. "Anyway, we had a family dinner the other night. Lachlan was fussing over Marisol and the baby, and Maggie had stars in her eyes for her new beau. Stella was on the sidelines. And for the first time, I saw hints that she wanted to join the game, but didn't know how. Especially when Ryan showed up."

"My grandson wants nothing to do with her," she snapped.

"You can't believe that." He fiddled with the handle of his coffee mug. "He looks at her like a man who wants *everything* to do with her."

She gritted her teeth. "He'd better not. Those two are not good for each other."

"I don't know, Gertie. They're adults. Lots of history behind them, sure, but it could be fixable—"

"It's not about their history, it's about their present! Neither of them needs what the other has to offer." And Ryan could be downright harmed by whatever was going on in Stella's life.

A tiny smile twitched at the corners of his mouth and he smoothed his beard.

Her heart skipped. *Oh, stop it. It did not. It's probably angina.*

"We appear to be on opposite sides of the field," he said.

They were. And she needed to change that. "You and your sports analogies. Does Carol hate them as much as Mary did?"

He leaned back in his chair. "Carol doesn't get to have an opinion on my speech peculiarities anymore."

"Oh?" Hope leaped in her chest. She'd never thought Tom's new woman worthy of his many charms. Silly, really. The pair had sounded well-suited.

Except Gertie preferred it when those charms were directed her own way. Not that she wanted to spend any of her precious few years left on romance. Too much of her life had been centered around keeping a man happy. But before Tom had left for Arizona, he'd made coming in for coffee part of his morning routine. And on the days when she helped out around the bakery, she'd enjoyed the five minutes that he'd focused all his attention on her.

Like now. His brown eyes fixed on her as if he was trying to figure out her secrets. Ha. Pointless, that quest. She didn't have secrets for him to discover.

Except for how much I enjoy his company...

"When I mentioned I wanted to come home for a spell to help out the grandkids, Carol took great offense to me canceling our trip to Europe. A river cruise, you know."

"I heard."

He smiled. "Of course, you did. Anyway, she didn't want to delay. And I can't blame her for that—obviously, guaranteed days are fewer when you're our age."

"You're young, compared to me," she commented. Tom was ten years younger than her own eighty-four.

"We're both doing all right, Gertie. And I've liked my time at the clinic these past months."

"You aren't disappointed about the cruise?" She yearned to travel, but the thought of dipping into her savings and ending up short for necessities—or accepting money from Ryan or her kids, like they'd offered many times over—gave her hives.

"Sure, I wanted to see the Danube," he said. "But I still had more to give to the clinic. I'll book something else once Maggie doesn't need me anymore."

"You're a good man, Thomas."

His eyes glinted. "I'm glad to be home. There are some things about Sutter Creek that I really missed."

Warmth crept up past the collar of her blouse and she folded her shaking hands. With any luck, he'd interpret her trembles as old age, not the excitement of someone who hadn't been flirted with in a long, long time. "There's a reason I've stayed put, you know. This place has my heart. Yours, too, I'd wager."

"You'd be right." He stared off into the distance for a second. "Stella would be a heck of a lot better off here than alone in the big city."

Darn it. She hadn't meant to provide him with a

reason to convince his granddaughter to stay for any length of time. Her nerves shifted from simple attraction to concern. Ryan had worked far too hard to establish himself as someone reliable and rooted, and Stella had brought not only their tumultuous past back with her, but also whatever ethical kerfuffle she was currently involved in at her firm.

"I'd better get to the clinic for my appointments." He paused, one eye squinting warily. "Would you like to have dinner with me, Gertrude?"

Her jaw dropped. "As in, a date?"

"Well, yes." That twitch of amusement again.

"Now why would we do that?"

Ryan entered the bakery in need of coffee. He'd successfully kept himself from seeking out Stella over the past few days, but that had meant covering for one of his deputies last night. He was lagging in the face of a city-council consultation and a bunch of paperwork that needed his signature.

His aunts' establishment was full of customers, as usual, and smelled like a vat of sugar.

Christ, he could bury his face in whatever was emitting that scent.

He waved at a few people, including Tom Reid and his grandmother, who were sitting at a table in the far corner. The veterinarian had always been a supporter of Ryan's, and greeted his gesture with a friendly smile.

Gran, however, didn't seem to be a fan of Tom

Reid's at the moment. Her brow was furrowed and she stared at Tom, lips firm and gaze disbelieving.

Oh, man. Her shenanigans were too much on a sleep-deprived morning. Jamming his hands into the pockets of his uniform jacket, he sidled up to the counter.

His aunt greeted him with a friendly hello and a latte in an extralarge to-go cup.

"You're a godsend, Aunt Nancy."

"It's on the house if you can find out whatever it is Dr. Tom's saying to put that look on Mom's face."

He shook his head. "My brain's not working this morning. I'm liable to say something completely off-color."

She passed him a pecan-streusel muffin in a small paper bag and fixed him with a look. "She's not going to talk to me about it. And she looks upset."

Ryan glanced back at his grandmother and stuck his nose in the open top of the bag. "That's what I was smelling. I need you to come over to my house and bake some of these so my kitchen smells like this."

She crossed her arms. "Recipe's in the book in the back. Bake your own damn muffins."

He cocked an eyebrow. "What if I suss out the source of Gran's consternation?"

"Oh, I can tell the source. I just can't figure out the specifics. She and Tom have always gotten along."

True. His grandmother might not be Stella's big-

gest fan, but she'd always had time for Dr. Reid. Unless the two were arguing *about* Stella…

Crap.

Staring at the ceiling for a couple of seconds, he
gathered his composure. Muffin in one hand and
coffee in the other, he sidled over to where the two
older folks were arguing.

"I just don't think that would be smart, Tom. What
would everyone think?"

Ryan gritted his teeth. He really disliked the idea
of his problems impacting his family, or Stella's, for
that matter.

"They'd think we were hungry, Gertrude," Tom
said.

Wait, what?

"Ryan, honey, stop hovering. Pull up a chair or
move along," Gran ordered.

Tom laughed. "He can take mine." The veterinarian stood, reaching across the table to squeeze Gran's
hand. Then he moved to the side. "I'm going to keep
asking, Gertie." He strolled toward the door, but not
before taking a second glance, brown eyes twinkling.

Ryan settled into the vacated seat and took a long
glug of coffee. "What was that about?"

"You're a sheriff, not a detective, dear," she said,
folding her hands on the table. She didn't have a
drink in front of her. A rag was folded neatly on the
corner to her left.

"Ouch," he said. "Gotta admit, I was glad you
were upset about something not involving me."

"I wasn't upset. I just wasn't about to have dinner with Tom Reid."

"Dinner?" He drew back. Gran hadn't mentioned wanting romance or companionship before. "Well… Why wouldn't you?"

"There's no point in that. I can't exactly pack up and fly off to the Danube."

"He wasn't asking you to go to the Danube. He was asking you out for steak or burgers or something."

She huffed a breath out her nose.

"But if you wanted to travel, you should do that, too," he added.

"I changed your diapers and wiped upchuck off your bedroom floor when you had too much beer out in Rafe's back forty. You don't get to tell me what to do."

"Telling, encouraging, six of one—"

"Ryan." Her mouth twisted, and the faint lines stood out around her pink painted lips. "This is better left alone. Both my friendship with Tom Reid and the idea of me gallivanting anywhere. You know full well my bank account doesn't allow irresponsibility like that."

He narrowed his eyes. "But if you want to do something, you should do it while you can."

"Thanks for the reminder of my mortality, dear."

"That's not what I meant."

"It's exactly what you meant."

He sighed. "Fine, it was, though it's one of my

least favorite thoughts. I have you pegged at making at least one hundred."

"Exactly why I need to be smart about my finances."

"Why don't you ask a financial planner?"

She sneaked a corner off his muffin and popped it in her mouth. "Nancy sure has a winner with this recipe."

He wasn't going to give up that easily. "You might find you can do more with your savings than you realize, Gran." An idea flashed into his head. They knew someone who was excellent with money. "You should talk to Stella."

She startled. "I beg your pardon?"

That obviously wasn't an actual request for him to repeat himself, but the grandmotherly equivalent of "The hell you say?" He waited, taking a long drink from his to-go cup.

"I couldn't possibly," she said, looking like she was about to crack a molar. "And if she's in some sort of trouble at work, I shouldn't be hiring her to dig into my finances."

Given he couldn't explain how he knew that wasn't a concern, this required a different angle. "Just think, you could pry to your heart's content while you were meeting. She'd never be the wiser." And maybe if Gran got a half hour to subtly prod Stella, she'd leave them be.

Lifting her chin at an imperious angle, she rose from her chair. "I'll consider it. And you should get back to work before you get fired for reasons having nothing to do with Stella Reid."

He laughed. "Will do, Gran." But he wasn't going to let her have the last word this time. Waving at his aunt, he cupped a hand around one side of his mouth. "He asked her out for dinner, Aunt Nancy."

He scooted outside before Gran could retaliate. He'd pay for that one at some point. But maybe if she was busy dealing with her own problems, she'd be too busy to pay attention to his.

Chapter Nine

"Are sheriffs allowed to gamble?"

A pair of long, jean-clad legs folded into the plastic chair next to Ryan, accompanied by that voice suited to singing slow, sexy ballads instead of managing a hedge fund. Oh, crap. What was Stella doing, sitting with him? Wednesday bingo was full of curious spies, including the small-but-mighty senior citizen sitting to his right. He kept his focus on his bingo card. "When the Rotary keeps their gambling license current, yeah."

"It's a public service," Gran interrupted, peering at Stella through her thick glasses. "He supervises me."

"Oh," Stella said cautiously. "You, uh, need help keeping up with the caller?"

"No. I cheat." The pink dauber flew across the grid of sixteen bingo cards almost autonomously.

Ryan ran a finger around the inside of the collar of his plaid shirt and dotted I 22 on the only one of his four cards with the drawn number. Wednesday-night bingo was a tradition for Gran and him. He got to shoot the breeze with town residents, and Gran liked the company. He smirked at her admission. It wasn't a total exaggeration—she did have a habit of trying to slip the occasional incomplete row past the caller.

"She can't be trusted," he said.

Stella's eyes flared, and he half expected her to come at him with an "apple doesn't fall from the tree" burn.

He watched her out of the corner of his gaze. "Going to join in?"

"Uh, yeah." A small stack of bingo cards fluttered in her hand. "Lach figured we should come join in and say thank-you in person to the organizing committee. It's lovely of them to put some of the proceeds toward our rebuilding costs. I was going to set up with my family…" Waving a hand at a table across the hall, she trailed off.

Lachlan had the baby in a carrier strapped to his chest; Marisol sat to his left. Maggie was with Asher, whose daughter must have been busy somewhere else, because the preteen was nowhere to be seen.

And Tom Reid finished up the fivesome. Leaving no chair for Stella.

She lifted her chin a little, gaze fixed on the caller.

"Full house tonight," he murmured apologetically.

"They're not used to leaving space for you," Gran said with a flurry of pink dots.

Stella pressed her lips together. "I figured that."

"Maggie shouldn't be out," Gran said. "Looks like she can't even hold a dauber with all those bandages."

"She's stubborn," Stella told her.

Ryan almost snorted. Stubborn? Ran in the family.

"Good thing your grandfather is home to take up the slack," Gran said.

The corners of Stella's mouth turned down. "That's why I'm here, too."

"Hmmm." Gran motioned to the table. "Spread your cards out, Stella."

His eyebrows flew up and he turned his head to his grandmother so that Stella couldn't see his incredulity. What was she getting at? With all her "you need to keep your distance" opinions, he'd expected her to shoo Stella away.

Gran met his silent question with an inscrutable expression. Maybe she figured bingo was platonic enough that the people around them wouldn't get the wrong idea.

"You can sit here, get caught up to where we

are," she continued. "With your magic with numbers, you'll probably beat us all."

Stella made four rows of four with the speed of a Vegas poker dealer. "You flatter me, Mrs. Rafferty."

"I never flatter, honey. In fact, I have some questions about investments, and Ryan pointed out that you'd be the person to ask."

"He did?"

"I'm not going to waste words by repeating myself. Now, I know your confidence got shook with this whole business problem you've run into—"

"I'm plenty confident. I didn't do anything wrong," Stella interrupted. "I'm just the source."

Gran stilled. "The source?"

"Oh, God," Stella whispered, blanching as white as her sweater. "Forget I said that. Please. I can't—"

"Gran won't say a word," he promised. "To *any-one*."

"I can keep quiet when I need to. You both should know that." Gran hummed again, attacking her cards with her dauber. "Will you help me?"

Stella unscrewed the cap on her purple dauber and efficiently filled in the calls she'd missed on the top row of her grid. "I'd be happy to help you, Mrs. Rafferty. Though I'm really not looking at getting into the personal-investment business."

"Isn't that what you're in?"

She shook her head. "Not exactly." Managing to keep up with current calls, she got the rest of her cards filled in faster than he'd thought possible.

"You are going to beat us," he said, nudging her with an elbow.

She startled and dropped her dauber. It rolled onto the ground.

They both leaned for it, ending up with faces close and hands fumbling for the plastic marker and almost entwining in the process. Her warm, minty breath caressed his cheek and her hair swayed sideways, brushing his shoulder.

And those eyes…

Heat spread low in Ryan's belly. *Ah, damn.*

His fingers closed over the dauber instead of running along her arm and testing the softness of her sweater, like they were clamoring to do. He straightened, passing her the marker.

She sat up, cheeks pink. "Thanks."

He tried to look away, but couldn't rip his gaze from the thrall of her blue irises.

She licked her lower lip with the tip of her tongue.

Something twinged inside him, a rusty creak of feelings long dead. And not worth reviving—she was leaving in a week and it would probably be another decade before she returned.

"Bingo!" Gran cried, waving her card over her head.

"Beats me every time," he lamented.

"No, she didn't," Stella said, looking puzzled.

He took another look at his cards. "Huh?"

Stella dragged a pink tipped finger diagonally

across one of his cards. "You had a bingo on the last call. You missed I 22 on this one. Half a game ago."

When you arrived. "Guess my mind was elsewhere."

"Uh, right." Her gaze darted between him and her family. He followed her line of sight to the other table. The Reids were laughing about something. Stella's siblings looked crazy comfortable with their partners. Romantic little smiles and touches.

He and Stella had never been content in that "worn-in flannel shirt" way. Sure, they'd shared smiles and a hell of a lot of touches. But they'd been passionate and obsessed and lustful—so many hallmarks of young, doomed love.

She gathered up her cards, hands rushed and fluttery. "I'll go see if they're planning to stay for a second game. Probably time for me to hit the road, though."

Good call. So why did something twist in his chest at the thought of her leaving? Hearts must have muscle memory, because there was no logical reason why he'd feel that way.

"When can we work on that financial advice?" his gran asked Stella.

"Tomorrow? I could meet you at the bakery for lunch."

Gran shook her head. "Too much of a fishbowl. Let's meet at Ryan's house."

"*Ryan's* house," Stella repeated suspiciously.

"My house?" he echoed.

"Well, coming over to the seniors' home won't work. I'd be getting questions from my friends for the next week," Gran said.

"Ryan's house it is," Stella agreed. "See you then." She nodded and left, heading in the direction of her family.

Damn it. Stella in his space... Clutching one of his coffee mugs and taking a sip with those sexy as hell lips. Sitting on his couch and leaving wisps of her scent on the microfiber fabric, so that the next time he went to take a nap, he'd be dreaming of holding her.

He waited until she was on the other side of the room before calling Gran on her nonsense. "How does inviting her over to my place make *any* sense?"

She lifted a shoulder.

"You're up to something."

"You said I got to pry. I figure the more she's out of her element, the better."

"She's completely out of her element here. Look at her." He nodded across the room, where Stella was saying goodbye to her family, posture awkward and expression forced-neutral. His heart panged. "She doesn't fit. Which is a good thing for me."

"She won't *let* herself fit. Entirely different. The key is figuring out if it would be possible to change her mind."

Ryan frowned, hearing the unsaid "and make sure that doesn't happen" in Gran's words. "Look, I don't want Stella affecting my job security any more than you do, but manipulating her is plain wrong."

"I wasn't thinking anything of the sort."

He groaned. Classic Gertie Rafferty. Which is what he hadn't wanted.

"Just listen to her financial advice. You're bored in Sutter Creek, and if you don't want to take money from the family to do some traveling, then you should figure out how to stretch your own dollars."

"Traveling…"

He caught her looking a little too long at the Reids, specifically in Dr. Tom's direction. Hmm. Maybe to get her out of his hair, he needed to match her interference with some of his own. "I tell you what. I'll help you with your fishing expedition."

"You will?"

"On one condition—you accept Tom's dinner invitation."

Her cheeks reddened. "Why would I do that?"

"Because you want to."

Which was excellent advice for his gran to take. He, on the other hand, needed to do the opposite.

"Where are you going?" Maggie asked, complaining in tone if not words. She was lounging on her sofa, as instructed by her surgeon, but Stella could tell she was beyond done with convalescing. Two months of burn treatments and skin-graft surgeries had taken a toll on her sister. "I'm so sick of my own company."

"You've been with me or Gramps every day since I got here, and Asher literally every minute he's not at work or playing chauffeur for Ruth. I'd have thought you were sick of having company."

Maggie shook her head. "You're not going to be here much longer, so I have to soak up your cheer while I can." She picked at a bandage. "Would you give up this whole 'staying at the hotel' thing, and come camp out in the second spare room? Please?"

Stella froze. Neither Maggie nor Lachlan had mentioned her sleeping arrangements since her initial argument with Lach. "You really want that?"

"Well, people are asking, and it's embarrassing."

"Oh." *There* was the truth.

Maggie made a face. "Don't look at me like that. I was trying to make it easy on both of us. You want the truth? I want you here. It's weird, because all we've ever had is distance, but…" She shrugged.

Stella could feel her mouth flapping but no matter how hard she tried to snap it shut, she couldn't. "I don't—"

"Just say yes."

"I—I guess I could check out of the hotel tomorrow." If Maggie wanted to pretend she was as close to Stella as she was to Lachlan, who was she to argue? They both knew, deep down, that their relationship would never be the same. But if Stella staying in the house helped Maggie's mindset, she'd heal faster. So the farce was worth it.

She checked her watch and collected her purse

from the kitchen, along with a fresh glass of water for Maggie. "Tell you what," she called to the other room. "As soon as I'm done with Gertie, I'll pick up pizza on the way home and we can share it with Gramps, Asher and Ruth. Vegetarian, I assume?" Maggie was vegetarian, and she'd mentioned that Asher stuck to as much of a kosher diet as he could.

"They like mushrooms," Maggie shouted back. "And Greek veggie for me."

She reentered the living room and handed her sister the glass. "Drink up. Fluids, remember? Speeds up the healing."

Maggie shot her a dry look. "Who's the doctor?"

A phrase that was becoming overused. "You are really doing an excellent job of living up to the maxim that doctors make the worst patients."

"Not sure that applies to veterinarians."

"It does with you."

"Jerk." But the insult lacked oomph. Fear flickered across her sister's pale face.

Stella sat at the other end of the couch, placing a hand on Maggie's velvety slipper. "What's wrong?"

"What if the grafting doesn't take? And physical therapy doesn't work? I mean, look at Asher's brother, Caleb. His hand surgeries didn't repair the avalanche damage, and he had to give up surgery..."

Stella's heart sank. Her sister had a lot of therapy ahead of her, and soon Stella would be back in New York, unable to be the support Maggie needed. "Want me to call Mrs. Rafferty to tell her I'll be a little late? I can stick around if you want to talk about it."

Maggie wiped away a tear. "I'm just being a baby."

"You're not. Career threats are a big deal." Of anyone, Stella would know.

"Stop. I don't want to talk about it."

"At all?" *Or with me?*

"Asher will be off work soon. If he hasn't run screaming from me unloading on him yet, he won't if I do it today. And he's bringing their dog over." Her face was a mix of misery and longing. "That'll help."

"You always did go to animals over people." Something inside her wanted to fix everything for Maggie, but Stella clearly wasn't the solution her sister wanted. She just needed to try harder.

"I've learned to reach out more," Maggie admitted.

"Asher's good for that?" She liked her sister's new man. Anyone who was able to debate the finer points of YA versus adult romance novels was good in Stella's book.

"Asher's *great* for that." Maggie waved a hand. "Aren't you going to be late? Go."

Oh, man, just when her sister was opening up a little, Stella had to leave. "I'm sorry I made plans."

Maggie sighed. "Really?"

"Yeah. This—" she motioned between them "—is nice. And new."

"A building fire puts things in perspective." Maggie narrowed her eyes and gingerly drew her blanket up to her chin. "What's it going to take for you, Stella? Is the threat to your job enough? I know you can't discuss whatever's going on at work, but that just makes me more concerned based on what's been on the news. I wish you'd let us support you."

"I'm here to help you, not to have you help me figure out my crap."

"No reason why it can't be both."

It was tempting to throw up a wall, but that wouldn't be fair. Not in the face of Maggie's raw honesty.

"Being open isn't easy."

Maggie snorted knowingly. "Better get used to it if you have a meeting with Mrs. Rafferty. She's going to grill you six ways to Sunday."

"Yeah, I dated her grandson for years. I remember. And I think I can match her."

Standing on Ryan's stoop ten minutes later, she wasn't feeling so confident.

Mainly because Gertie hadn't answered the door—Ryan had. He was hunched over a little, holding the collar of a roly-poly Labrador, who stared at Stella with mild interest.

Ryan was wearing that black uniform shirt again. It set off his eyes just right. And it would be way too easy to greet him with a kiss.

She settled on "Oh. You're here."

He looked at her like she was missing a good part of her frontal cortex. "It's my house."

"Yeah, but I thought you'd be at work."

He let go of the dog, who, after a cursory sniff, waddled off to her bed, having deemed Stella unworthy.

Gertie would be so proud of her great-granddog.

Backing up, he waved Stella in. "Technically, I'm in my office right now. Can't you tell?" He smiled, a devastating curve of lip and flash of teeth that melted her insides. "Thought you might want a referee, though. Gran will be here any minute."

"So we're alone," she murmured, zipping out of her leather ankle boots. Losing the height took her down a few inches. He'd always been too tall for his own good, but just right for Stella. Being a tall woman meant she had to savor her moments of feeling feminine, delicate. But around Ryan, it was the physical reality. And she'd missed having the option of being carried around like a featherweight.

He'd still be able to do that. Those arm muscles didn't lie—

"Stop looking at me like that," he said gruffly.

She swallowed, hoping to cover up how dry her mouth had gotten. "Like what?"

"You know."

"I do not."

He took a step toward her. "Stella," he warned.

"What?"

"You're lying."

Crap. There was no hiding anything from him.

She lifted her hands, palms up. "Fine. I was looking at you *like that*."

He stepped forward again, until only a foot of space separated them. "See, this is why I didn't want you over at my house."

His hands landed on her waist, and she shivered as the weight of his touch settled, as if they hadn't been separated for almost two decades.

She slid her palms up his chest, over his uniform shirt. "You didn't?"

He shook his head, and backed her up until her shoulders pressed into the door and her body tucked into his. "I knew I'd have to do this."

His lips brushed hers. A tease of a kiss. She grumbled a complaint and jammed her fingers into his hair, pulling his mouth closer, meeting his tentative test with all the pent-up frustration she'd been holding inside for the last week.

Week. Months. Eighteen years...

He groaned and tasted her deeply. His hands roamed up her sides, and she pressed into his big, muscular body, needing the friction of more than lips and tongues.

"Christ, Stella—"

"Those better be prayers of thanks, honey," said a voice from somewhere behind Ryan. "Because if anyone but me saw you doing that you'd be in up to your neck in trouble."

He stepped back, cursing low. "Hi, Gran."

Stella pressed a hand to the bottom of her rib cage

and tried to take a steadying breath before Gertie Rafferty recognized just how much that kiss had thrown her. Holy crap, Ryan could kiss...

"Since when do you come in the back door?" he asked his grandmother, who stood by the kitchen island with her arms crossed.

"Wouldn't have been able to get in the front door anyway, not with the two of you using it for hanky panky," she said. She sat primly at the dining-room table tucked into the space between the front door and the kitchen. Ryan's house was small, but cozy. *And you'd probably be in the bedroom by now were it not for Gertie.*

Stella didn't know if she was annoyed or relieved at the interruption. Smoothing her hands down her sweater and lifting her chin, she sat across from the older woman. "Let's talk money."

"We have all day to do that. What's more important is what I just saw."

"We're not errant teens anymore," Ryan interjected, walking to his fridge and grabbing a few sodas. He set a Diet Coke in front of Stella—damn it, he had way too good of a memory for Stella's preferred beverages—and passed Gertie a ginger ale. "Respectfully? Back off."

"How can I? You're losing perspective. Someone has to keep it."

"Stella and I have plenty of perspective," he murmured.

"And is it taking into account whatever she did at

work? When the news of that comes out, and people actually have facts instead of the current rumors, what's going to happen then?"

"It'll exonerate Stella," he snapped, sitting down at the end of the table.

He sounded so certain. His confidence warmed her belly, even if he couldn't know more than the vague details being reported. Unless... Had he gone back on his word and investigated her?

Her stomach clenched. "Why are you so sure?"

He stared at her, his soft expression revealing no clues. "I trust you. That's enough for me." Emotion shimmied in her chest.

"Probably shouldn't have so much blind faith, Sheriff," she croaked.

Gertie jabbed him in the arm. "People trusting *you* is the bigger issue. And you can't be involved with a woman who's involved in a crime," the older woman insisted. She pierced Stella with her gaze. "Did you break the law?"

Stella met Gertie's challenge. The truth burbled beneath the surface, and she scrambled to hold back any detail that would violate her agreement with the investigators. "I haven't committed a crime since I drove your brother-in-law's car, knowing full well it was stolen."

"Stella," Ryan said quietly, staring at his tented fingers. "You don't need to explain yourself."

Dog claws clicked on the floor and Ryan's dog nosed her head into Stella's lap. Stella dug her fingers into the lab's soft fur and breathed until her pulse slowed. Calmer, she had a better grasp of what needed to be said.

"As for whether Ryan's shining reputation will be tarnished by the likes of me, it's all moot," she pointed out, still focused on Gertie. She couldn't look at him, not when his eyes shone with faith and respect. She patted her lap, inviting the dog to drape across her legs. She looped her arms around the dog's chunky neck and hugged the canine close. "One kiss does not a rekindled relationship make. Soon enough, I'll go back to New York. And Ryan will be able to stay here and marry goddamn Emma Halloran—"

Ryan's tender expression darkened.

"If only," Gertie muttered under her breath.

Stella narrowed her eyes. "Do you want my help with your finances or not?"

"I do, actually." The older woman almost sounded contrite.

With the conversation focused on money and investments, the pressure in Stella's chest eased. With Puddle full-on snoring in her lap, she spent enough time building a picture of Gertie's finances that Ryan had to leave before they were done.

"I'll call you," he said.

"Don't feel you have to," Stella replied mildly as the dog scrambled down to say goodbye to her alpha human.

"I'll *call you*," he repeated, shaking his head as he left through the front door.

Stella stared at it closing for a second too long.

"He's my most precious person, you know," Gertie said, clenching her hands around the thin scarf she'd removed from her neck.

He used to be mine. Nodding, she cleared her throat. "I think we can identify areas where your money could be working better for you. If you make some adjustments, you'll have enough to create an annual travel fund."

Gertie studied her for a moment, as if trying to decide if she was going to call out Stella on the subject change. "If that's what I decide to do with it. My family is used to me being here."

"Yeah, I've found that when you leave, people adjust." Oh, damn. She closed her eyes, chest tightening. "Sorry. I didn't mean it that way. No one would ever forget you, Gertie."

Mrs. Rafferty's mouth twisted. "No one forgot you, either, Stella. Even if you hoped we would."

Chapter Ten

Working on the barn every day until the following Tuesday was oddly soothing. Maggie was easing back into some of her veterinary duties, Gramps was supporting her and Lach was juggling his vet-tech hours with his responsibilities at the training school. Stella didn't have much construction experience, but she could wield a paint roller. With the majority of the drywalling completed during the work bee, there were plenty of surfaces to slap with paint.

The solitude was welcome, too. Staying at Maggie's since Friday meant a whole lot of socializing in the evenings, exactly the time of day she was used to having space. So she didn't bother with putting in her earbuds and catching up on podcasts while she painted—the sound of eggshell latex slicking over the walls was meditative, counteracting how jittery she'd been since that kiss.

More than jittery. *Consumed.*

He'd stayed away, at least. Somehow, they'd managed to avoid each other. She'd spent most of her time with her half siblings, which had likely helped, but still. Not running into someone in Sutter Creek for five days seemed noteworthy.

"Stella?"

The low voice startled her, and she almost dropped the roller. "Did I *summon* you?" she muttered.

Ryan rounded the corner into the conference room, concern shadowing his eyes. He had on his uniform, including his black cowboy hat. Great. One more hot mental image to fixate on.

He came right up to her, lifting his hand and almost touching her face. He dropped it to his side before he actually made contact. "Are you okay?"

"Do I not look okay?"

"Yeah, but you're good at putting on a show."

Fear rolled through her. "What happened?"

"You haven't seen the story yet?"

Her stomach bottomed. That she'd had close to two weeks before the news broke had been both a blessing and a curse. She'd known this day was coming. But she still didn't want to face it. "I left my phone in my purse. How bad is it?"

He held out his phone.

She shook her head. "My hands are covered in paint. Just tell me."

"It names you. And it speculates that you took a deal to cover up something you did. Mentions a multi-agency investigation."

Her knees shook, and she sank to the cement floor, cross-legged. *Oh, God...*

Ryan took the paint roller out of her hand, placed it in the tray and kneeled next to her. "Hey. Deep breaths."

"Yep." Impossible, what with the knowledge that she might never get her life back, her *dream* back.

He stroked her back. "Seriously, breathe."

"I am," she croaked. Not well, though. And she did not need an audience judging her wheezes. "Why are you here?"

"When Special Agent Gill couldn't get a hold of you, he called me to see if I'd check up on you."

She jerked away from his touch. "You know my FBI contact?"

He nodded curtly. "He called me the day after you got to town."

What? "How much do you know?"

His hand returned to her back, a comforting weight. If she scooted closer and leaned on him, shared her burdens with him, could she trust him?

Yes or no, it won't do any good in the long run. She'd be returning to New York to deal with the trial and rebuilding her career alone. Better to start out how she intended to continue.

Ryan stayed silent a few more seconds before replying. "I know enough to understand that these news stories are false. But I didn't need a federal agent's explanation in order to believe your innocence."

"So you've been sitting on the truth since I got here? And you didn't tell me?"

He kissed her temple. "Couldn't. I'd think you'd understand that."

Anger sizzled in her veins. *How could he not... No. Be honest.* She wasn't mad at Ryan. He'd followed protocol, just like she had. And letting her devastation spill out onto him, hot and furious, would be exceedingly unfair. "Well, you can let Agent Gill know I'm fine. Or better yet, I'll call him myself. I'm going to need to get a hold of my lawyers, too. They've probably been trying to contact me."

"Okay." His brow furrowed. "But I'd like to support you through this."

What she would have given for him to say that eighteen years ago... Then blurred with now, current accusations and Ryan's past desertion swirling in her belly like when she'd stirred the paint in the tray. She shot him a glare. "Forgive me if I don't understand that. The last time I needed you—and my God, I really did, Ryan, more than you know—you didn't even have the guts to face me in person. So do me a favor...walk away again. Please. You don't need my drama, and whatever *support* you were hoping to give? It's not the kind I'm looking for."

His head hung for a second. "Right. I'm not going to force you to accept comfort. Even though we both know you need it."

"No, I don't."

"Hurting alone? It's unnecessary, Stella. Call if you change your mind. I mean it." Standing, he tipped his hat, then left.

And she spent the rest of the day pretending the nausea consuming her body was from dealing with the news report, not from the yearning look he shot her before he disappeared out the door.

At about seven, Maggie and Gramps forced her to mute her phone, which had been blowing up with social-media alerts and emails for hours, and leave the house for dinner. She still wasn't able to give her family details about the evidence she'd be providing, but the investigators had at least given her permission to tell them that the allegations about her taking a plea were unfounded. As for the rest of the world, stories were running, wild and unchecked.

"You've done what you can, dear," Gramps said, pouring the three of them glasses of water from the milk bottle that served as a water pitcher at the hole-in-the-wall pie restaurant Maggie had insisted they go to. "Have something to eat."

Stella clutched her napkin and glanced at the people sitting at the next table over. She was pretty sure she'd gone to high school with them. And they were doing a terrible job of pretending they weren't talking about her.

"I had a big lunch," she lied.

"You painted through lunch," Maggie said. She held her cutlery awkwardly, given her wound dressings.

"You kept track?" Stella challenged. She wasn't used to people monitoring her like this. And the extra eyeballs on her personal life, added to the national-level scrutiny about her job, weighed on her like an iron net.

Maggie shrugged. "I can see the barn from my office."

"Good to know."

The bell on the door jingled and two vaguely familiar woman walked in, bundled up in winter gear and knit hats.

Maggie lifted a hand. "Emma! Georgie! Hey!"

Stella's blood boiled. The famous Emma, and her mom. She could see why everyone thought Emma and Ryan would suit each other. With her bright smile, dark brown ponytail and a mountain-chic puffy jacket, the woman could have been a model for Sutter Creek tourism advertisements. And her mom looked as sharp as anything, gaze honed in on Stella.

They made their way over to the table, Emma smiling apologetically.

"Hey, hon," she said to Maggie. "Good to see you out of the house. Ready for a girls' night out soon?"

"Sure," Maggie said. "I'll bring Stella."

"Oh." Emma's green eyes widened. "Uh, okay. So…you're staying longer, Stella?"

"We'll see," she replied tightly. Agent Gill had told her not to return to Manhattan yet. But even so, she wasn't about to force her company on someone who didn't want her around.

"Any news on the thefts, Georgie?" Gramps asked.

"Not yet. Seems our sheriff's attention has been pulled elsewhere recently." Georgie crossed her arms over her purple Gore-Tex jacket.

Before Stella could protest that everyone needed to back off and let Ryan do his job, Gramps sat back in his chair and said, "Now, I'm not sure how fair that is."

"It's plenty fair," the older woman said. "Every time I've gone to look for him, he's been involved with something to do with a Reid."

Gramps chuckled. "We elected him, too." He sobered. "I'm sorry you're not getting the answers you want, though. Do you really think the investigation is hitting snags because Sheriff Rafferty isn't being thorough?"

"I don't know." Georgie frowned. "He does seem distracted. Today, especially. We had a meeting this afternoon and I didn't know it was possible for a person to check a phone that many times in fifteen minutes. I just hope he isn't reverting to the kind of shoddy decision-making he was known for when he was younger."

Nobody looked at Stella. They didn't need to. She felt their judgment, anyway. Flames licked her face.

"Excuse me for a second," she said, then grabbed her purse and headed for the washroom. She ran her hands under cold water and pressed them to her hot cheeks. "Come on," she told her reflection in the mirror over the sink. "Hold it together. You can handle one passive-aggressive ranch owner."

She pulled her phone out of her pocket. Her heart sank at the notification screen that was too full to display all the messages she'd gotten. Requests for interviews. More accusations from coworkers. Links to articles and videos sent by the few people who probably thought they were being supportive by giving her a heads-up. After pressing the power button, she dropped the device back in her purse and returned to the table.

Small miracles—Emma and Georgie were up at the counter. Her pulse settled a bit.

Maggie wore an apologetic frown. "Not sure what's gotten into Georgie."

"Sounds like logical business-owner concerns to me," Stella said. "I didn't realize how serious the thefts were."

"Ryan didn't mention it?" Maggie sounded surprised.

"No. I've only seen him once since Thursday, even if people think we're living in each other's pockets again." *Nor did I take the time to ask what's going on in his life.* She could tell herself it was because she wasn't interested in getting close to him again. But in actuality, it was also due to her being too focused on her own crap to consider any of his. Guilt crept up her neck and she sighed. "Gertie was right about people being concerned about his involvement with me."

Maggie rolled her eyes. "Georgie is just one person."

"I get the sense that more people are talking about me than Georgie," Stella said.

Gramps coughed. "I've heard some gossip."

"Today?" If her grandfather, who was known for being oblivious to that sort of thing, was hearing rumors, then they must be rampant.

"No, at the bakery last week."

"Damn it." The iron net doubled in weight. She took an extralarge breath to try to hold off the feeling of suffocation, but it didn't work. She needed space. Living at Maggie's was the opposite of that. But she couldn't go back to holing up in the hotel—that would be too hurtful. "I need somewhere I can get away. Where I'm not causing problems for Ryan, and where I can't keep checking my phone."

A thoughtful expression crossed Gramps's face. "There's my fishing cabin."

Maggie guffawed. "You? At the cabin? There's no Starbucks there. And when was the last time you lit a propane stove?"

Stella glared at her. "I'm not incompetent. I can use matches." Her sister had a point on the Starbucks, though. But if she wanted isolated, that cabin, out in the middle of the woods, would certainly fit the bill. "Is it decently winterized?"

Gramps's silver-white eyebrows rose. "Yes. Wouldn't suggest it if it wasn't."

Even the possibility of being cut off from everything eased the pressure in her chest. "Would you take me out there?"

"If that's what you want," he said.

She *wanted* her old life back. But in the absence of that, maybe a few days to recalibrate out at Gramps's cabin would be perfect. "Let's go in the morning."

True to his word, her grandfather took her out early the next day, him on his old snowmobile and her on a borrowed one from Maggie. A light snow fell while they traveled, lending the forest a romantic vibe. She had enough supplies to last a week, though he promised to come check on her in two days. Gramps showed her how to use the woodstove, turned on the propane for her and got the fridge and stove going, then pointed her in the direction of the outhouse and asked her one last time if she was okay to be alone. She assured him she was, and then he was gone.

Oh, man. She hadn't been out here in two decades. She and Ryan had sneaked out for an overnight once. During the summer, though, and on an ATV, not a snowmobile. They'd spent most of the time in the nearby lake. And when they'd come in to warm up, they made a cozy nest on the double bed in the one bedroom.

She could sleep on the couch then. She wasn't spending the night with the memory of Ryan's eager, fumbling hands bringing her pleasure. She sank onto the brown Naugahyde couch. Then again, they'd fooled around on the couch, too. And he'd kissed her in the teeny kitchen.

Okay, she really hadn't calculated well. In her haste to get out of town, she'd forgotten that this was one place that had only witnessed good times. And she missed those good times, damn it. How was she supposed to clear her head when all she could think about was him wistfully telling her he wished they could stay in the woods forever?

Growling at herself for not taking all that into consideration *before* saying goodbye to her grandfather, she tried to stay busy. Making herself tea and soup and reading a well-loved Beverly Jenkins novel she found buried on one of the bursting-at-the-seams shelves kept her occupied until dark. Her second day wasn't much different.

"Should I be concerned that I've started talking to myself? Nah." She cut into the omelet she'd made for dinner on the small, four-burner propane stove that was older than she was, and pretended the pangs in her stomach were from hunger, not loneliness. And then the wind started blowing.

Her pulse picked up. "I'm fine. This is what I wanted. To be alone. Not causing trouble for anyone, following the plan." Needing to use the facilities, if one could call an old wooden outhouse that, she put on her parka and the snowmobiling boots she'd borrowed from Maggie and opened the door. A gust of wind smacked into her, along with a face full of snowflakes. A foot of powdery snow had accumulated on the path. She paused on the wooden stoop, nerves jangling. Pointing her flashlight down the short path to the outhouse, she could barely see through the swirling white. "A *blizzard*. Awesome," she muttered. This was not the six to twelve inches that had been forecast.

"No whining," she reminded herself. "You're a grown-ass woman, and you asked to come here."

She did her business, and made sure to bring a shovel inside with her in case she had to dig a path in the morning before settling in for the night.

Morning rolled around. Her joints ached from being curled up on the ancient couch.

Maybe tonight she'd brave the bedroom.

She stoked the embers of the fire back into flame, got it roaring and went to use the outhouse. The wind wasn't rattling the windows anymore, which was welcome. Swinging the door open, she stopped short. Her jaw dropped. Close to three feet of snow barricaded her in.

Find the bright side, find the bright side... "At least I brought in the shovel."

Ryan rolled his stiff neck. Six o'clock, and his Friday shift was finally ending. He threw on his coat and clicked off his office light, locking up behind him. He had the weekend off, and after being up all night dealing with a horrible accident on the highway to West Yellowstone and monitoring all the minor, snow-related complaints in town today, he intended to use every second to relax.

What would Stella be up to? He hadn't seen her since Tuesday. It had felt oddly incomplete. Ridiculous, given he'd gone his entire adult life without her. *Though maybe my life wasn't complete...*

His phone rang as he was climbing into his truck. He narrowed his eyes at the number. "Dr. Tom? What can I do for you?"

The veterinarian sighed with what sounded like relief. "Glad I caught you, son. Is this a bad time?"

Ryan's heart clenched at the endearment. Tom Reid probably threw it around like candy off a parade float, but the kid lurking inside Ryan's hollow places soaked up the affection. He'd never gotten that kind of attention from his dad. Even his grandpa had been brusque. Once upon a time, he'd wondered if he'd get to call Tom "Gramps," but that was long gone. He'd take the "son," though. "Good a time as any. What's on your mind?"

"Stella."

Ryan held in a groan. "People still harassing her about the media accusations?" He'd had to warn more than one person who was taking Stella's story out of context.

"Not to her face. They can't. She's at the cabin."

"*Your* cabin?" A brief flash of Stella's naked limbs

on a plaid camp blanket burned on his brain before he shut it off. *"Why?"*

"She wanted space. But neither of us expected the snow."

Shivering, he turned on his truck and cranked the heat. "No one did. Does she have enough food and water? And fuel?"

"She should. But I was supposed to go out there and check on her today. And I wasn't able to—I got stuck out at Rafe Brooks's place with Lachlan. And now it's late, and my eyes aren't the best at night. Setting out on the trail… I just don't think I can do it. But I hate to think of her sitting there alone, worried about why I didn't come."

He hated thinking of her out there alone, too. For entirely different reasons. Mainly to do with that flash of memory, and wishing he could experience it one more time.

Safety, Rafferty. Focus on her safety.

"She wouldn't assume it was because of the snow?"

"She might. But she might also wonder if I'd gotten hung up somewhere, and try to come find me. She could get lost, or worse…"

Genuine concern laced Tom Reid's words.

The thousand search-and-rescue calls he'd witnessed during his time with the sheriff's department didn't lie—things could go sideways in the woods but quick. He caught his toes starting to tap. Damn it. He wouldn't be able to relax tonight, not without knowing Stella was safe.

"Would you be able to take Puddle for the night if I go?"

"Certainly."

"It's a deal," Ryan said. "I'll check on Stella."

"Tonight?"

"Yeah, I know that trail like the back of my hand. I'll bring the dog by and then head out."

Two hours later, backpack slung over his shoulder and ice from yet more precipitation crusted to his neck warmer, he peered through the foggy glass on the front door of the Reid cabin. He didn't see any movement, but at least a light was on.

He knocked.

"Who's there?" Stella's suspicious tone was clear, even through the door.

"Stella? It's Ryan. Your grandfather asked me to check on you."

A shadow shifted through the glass. "I have a weapon. Prove it's you."

He had a weapon, too—he'd strapped his shoulder holster under his heavy snowmobiling jacket before he left the house—but he wasn't about to announce that. "The night we got arrested, you told me you didn't want to love me anymore."

The lock clicked and the door opened a crack, then all the way.

Her face was clouded with fury, like the snow clouds overhead, not that he could see them for the dark. But the storm was picking up again, and he knew what the sky looked like when troubled.

"You scared the bejesus out of me. I knew it wasn't Gramps because your snowmobiles sound different. I had visions of you being an ax murderer," she snapped, pulling the edges of her fuzzy cardigan closed in front of her chest. "Why are you *here*?"

"Your grandfather asked me to check on you. He wasn't able to get out here today, so he sent me instead."

She narrowed her eyes and still didn't invite him in. "Well, you checked on me. Now you can go."

"Go? Stella, doll—"

"I'm *not* your doll."

"Sorry. But the temperature's dropping, and more snow's coming. The visibility's garbage, and I slept all of two hours last night. It'd be dangerous for me to head back tonight."

"So why'd you come out then? Wasn't that dangerous, too?"

"Probably." He shrugged. "I needed to see you were okay."

Her mouth gaped, then slammed shut. She whirled and stormed over to the couch. "Do what you want. Take the bedroom. I haven't been using it."

Shutting the front door behind him, he stripped out of his gear and hung the wet pieces on the laundry line behind the potbellied stove. The cabin was cozy and warm, despite the storm. It smelled like the wood fire and some sort of savory food, maybe sausages. A half-full mug of what looked like tea sat next to a romance novel on the coffee table, and the couch was made up like a bed. He faced her. "You sure you don't want the bed?"

"Yes," she said, teeth gritted. Her gaze flicked to his shoulder holster and her pupils flared a little.

"Occupational habit," he explained.

"Wasn't wondering."

Wondering, maybe not. But enjoying? Looked to be so. Her cheeks were pink in the warm glow of the propane lights.

Seating was limited in the tiny cabin. The couch barely classified as a three-seater, but it looked way more comfortable than the pair of vintage vinyl chairs tucked under the small kitchen table. He sat next to her and held his hands in the direction of the stove to warm them. "I'm sorry I disturbed your peace. But I couldn't let your grandfather worry." *I wouldn't have slept a wink myself.*

"Okay. But your whole 'I can get here, but I can't get home,' is utterly illogical."

He smiled. "There's calculated risk, and then there's senseless."

She burrowed into her sleeping bag, inching as far from him as she could get without falling over the arm of the damn couch. "The boy I knew was all about senseless risk."

Wincing, he leaned back and shook his head. "I was." Every cell of his body wanted to pull her against him. But her cocoon act suggested she wanted none of that.

Or she *did* want him, and was desperately throwing up physical barriers. *Hmm.* "If the past couple weeks haven't shown you that I've changed, I don't know what will."

"I don't know what will, either. And I'm going to tuck in. Do whatever floats your boat."

He chuckled, easing to his feet and making his way to the bedroom. "And if 'floating my boat' includes a kiss good-night?" he called over his shoulder.

"Then you're going to sink."

Chapter Eleven

On Saturday morning, Gertie huffed at her phone as her call went to voice mail for the third time. Where was Ryan? She'd come to the bakery for her weekly tea-and-scone chat with her book club, had even stayed for an hour after they finished discussing the latest rom com to take the bestseller list by storm. Not even a hint of her grandson.

Actually, that wasn't true. A half-dozen people had asked after him, thinly veiled questions about his job and his love life. But no sign of the man himself.

Well. She'd just need to go by his house, then. Make sure he was okay.

She took her cup and plate back to the dishwasher and called a hasty goodbye to Vivian, who was running the till. Checking her phone again to see if Ryan had called back, she exited the swinging doors and promptly collided with a tall, fit body.

"Oh, I'm so sorry, I was looking at my phone. I'm as bad as a high schooler—" Her breath caught as she took in just who that body belonged to. "Tom. Good morning."

He grinned, teeth as white as the carefully groomed shock of hair on his head. He put two breakfast sandwiches down on the nearest table. He unzipped his green ski jacket, then slung it over the back of one of the two chairs.

He had on ski pants, too.

She wouldn't mind taking a ride up the gondola if it meant catching a glimpse of Tom carving turns down the mountain.

"Headed up the hill?" she asked, voice wavering a little. Her pulse skipped. Embarrassment pricked the back of her neck.

"That I am. Convinced Lachlan to ski with me for the afternoon. It's hard to pull him away from the baby, but the snow is unreal after that blizzard." He motioned to his grandson, who was at the counter putting in an order.

"Hmm. Maybe that's where Ryan is," she mused aloud.

Tom cocked an eyebrow and sat. "Not unless he and Stella came back from the cabin at first light."

She froze. "What cabin?"

"Mine," he said.

Her brain stuttered. Stella and Ryan had gone out to Tom's fishing cabin? "That doesn't make sense." Or did it? She *knew* that kiss she'd walked in on would lead to no good. If the two of them had up and escaped to get some privacy, that could mark the beginning of the end of Ryan's election hopes. Her stomach turned, and she looked at Tom, not bothering to hide her confusion. "He didn't tell me he was—" She cut herself off as Lachlan arrived at the table with two steaming mugs.

He set one down in front of his grandfather and kept one for himself. "Didn't realize you'd be joining us, Mrs. Rafferty, or I'd have asked you what you wanted."

"Thank you, dear, but I'm not staying, I…" She didn't know *what* to do.

Tom studied her, concern in his eyes. "I asked Ryan to go check on her last night."

Wait, *he'd* asked? Her ears started buzzing, and she stared at him, unable to pick her chin off her chest. Tom added some sort of explanation about getting stuck working and worrying about Stella in the blizzard and his night vision, but all she heard was his first words on a loop. *I asked Ryan.*

"You did *what*?"

His brow furrowed and he reached for her hand. The warmth of his fingers chased away the chill in hers, and she almost let herself enjoy it, except he had thrown her grandson and Stella into a shoebox of a cabin together overnight, and how *dare* he? She yanked her hand away.

"I was honestly worried about Stella," he explained, the corners of his mouth turning down.

"I could have gone," Lachlan pointed out.

"*He* could have gone," Gertie echoed.

Tom's frown slowly shifted into a resigned smile. "But then it wouldn't have forced Stella and Ryan into a tiny room, hopefully compelling them to talk out everything that's gone unsaid between them."

Lachlan snorted.

Gertie had to unlock her jaw, she'd been clenching her teeth so hard. "Did they *want* your interference?"

A guffaw rang through the bakery as Tom cracked up, almost doubling over with laughter. "*My* interference? You're something else, Gertie Rafferty."

"You can't possibly—" She braced her hands on her hips "I mean, I haven't—"

"Yes, you have. You've been poking your nose into Ryan's business since he was sixteen and actually needed to know someone cared enough to take an interest in what he did."

"And you think he doesn't now?"

She chanced a look at Lachlan, who was pretending not to listen. A laugh was still dancing on his lips. Impertinent, just like Ryan.

But Tom Reid was the worst offender of the bunch.

Backing away a step, she held up a finger and glared at the handsome veterinarian. "If this ends up being bad for my grandson, I'm blaming you."

"Blame away," Tom said cheerfully. "I'm betting it'll be nothing but good for the both of them."

"I hope you're right. And… Don't break anything while you're skiing today." Lifting her chin, she turned and headed for the door.

"You know, while we're on the topic of things that could be good for Raffertys," Tom called at her back, "my invitation for dinner still stands."

"And I might have said yes, had it not been for this nonsense." She left the bakery before she gave in to temptation and changed her mind.

Stella woke up on the couch with a shiver. *Ugh.* She should have taken the perennial fairy-tale advice to stay out of the forest—nothing good ever happened in little cabins in the woods.

Weren't sleeping bags supposed to be warmer than this? Her toes were approaching icicle range, even inside her thermal socks. *You know where it would be warm? In an actual bed. Even better— with a big, bulky sheriff to share body heat with.* She growled at her misguided inner voice. Ryan was already disturbing her external peace. He didn't get to commandeer her thoughts, too. Until she could get him packed up and out the door, she'd have to keep him at arm's length.

Staring down the heavy stove, she willed it to relight. Damn lack of magical powers. Her attempts to break out both a spell and to use the Force hadn't worked yesterday, either. Nor had she figured out a way to stay in her sleeping bag without falling on her face while kindling the fire back to life. She was about to brave the frigid air when even-gaited footsteps emerged from the back bedroom.

She squeezed her eyes shut. Delaying "good morning" seemed to be the smartest option.

Metal squawked on metal, which had to be the door of the stove being opened. Then the crumpling of newspaper, the thwap of kindling being settled into place, the snick of a match.

Lifting one lid a fraction, she watched Ryan's fire-building technique.

Fine, she watched his shoulders. Hello, glorious breadth—the red-and-black plaid shirt he had on was either the one she'd spotted in the bedroom closet or identical to it. Either way, the thick flannel fit just right across his broad, muscled back.

"Where's your holster?" she grumbled. That had fit him just right, too. She'd told herself she abhorred firearms for years. But the minute Ryan ambled in last night, armed and in protector mode, an ache settled at the apex of her thighs and it still hadn't faded.

He angled his head just enough to look at her out of the corner of his eye. "I don't sleep with it on. And I trust you're not going to steal it."

"Did you get that shirt from the closet?"

"I needed an extra layer. Is that a problem?"

Only that I want to take it off you. "No. Unless it smells like old fish."

He plucked the material between two fingers and brought it to his nose. "Nope. Cedar chest."

"Great," she grumbled. Add that to his outdoorsy, Yankee-candle smell? She'd be holding back from rubbing her face against the soft material until he left.

Warmth drifted over from the growing fire. He added a few logs and straightened, leaving the stove door open.

"Is that safe?" she asked.

"Just until it catches. Want to come warm up?"

She pulled her sleeping bag into a tighter hood around her face. "I'm toasty already."

He snorted. "Not sure why I expected you to be less irritable after a night's sleep." After throwing on his coat and boots, he left for a few minutes. When he returned, he stripped off his outerwear—giving her a peek of a six-pack that proved the good sheriff did not skip ab day—and crossed the small room to the corner that served as a kitchen. He started making coffee and busying himself poking through the cupboards.

"I'm not irritable," she said quietly. "It's more… testy."

"Whatever synonym makes you happy, Stella." He started nosing through the cupboards. "What were you planning to eat for breakfast?"

"I dunno, toast?"

"That's a sad lack of imagination." He set a pot and a cast-iron pan on the stove. "I'm not here to wreck your day. In fact, I should be complaining that it's my weekend being interrupted."

"Should?"

He cast her a rueful smile. "Being holed up in a cozy cabin with a beautiful woman checks off almost all the boxes on my 'how to spend a day off' list."

Don't ask, don't ask— "Almost?" *Damn it.*

His mouth curled up in a knowing, enigmatic half smile.

"Urgh, *you.* You know that would be a terrible idea, right?"

"I was just referring to the weather. Might be a tricky trip back home, is all."

Yeah, right. Snowmobiling concerns did not put that suggestive look on his face. "Need help with breakfast?"

He brought her a coffee. "Nah. We can eat toast another day, Stella. I'll take care of this one."

She warmed her hands with her mug, tromped to the outhouse and returned to a warm cabin full of savory, spicy smells.

He ladled his creation into two of her grandfather's blue enamel bowls.

Curiosity piqued, she went into the kitchen and peered around his shoulder. "What are you up to?"

"Feeding you, Bella."

She stiffened. "What is this, pull out the insipid, rhyming nicknames day? 'Cause I can assure you, I'm not about to revert to 'Ry-guy.'"

He lifted a shoulder and motioned for her to sit

at the old Formica table, then set a steaming serving of noodles and broth in front of her. A poached egg crowned the creation, dotted with some sort of diced, fried meat and the green onion she'd brought to go on a salad.

She eyed him. "Ramen? For breakfast?"

"You're living in New York. You can't tell me you haven't eaten noodles first thing in the morning." Settling in across from her, he tucked into his serving, humming with satisfaction.

He used to make that face after he made her see stars.

Cheeks heating, she poked the egg yolk with a fork so it broke, oozing golden yellow. She spun a mouthful with her fork and spoon and took a bite. Oh, wow. Umami and salt with the perfect kick.

"I see what you did here. You were trying to prove a point," she said, shoveling in another bite.

He smiled cockily. "Maybe."

"What are the meat bits?"

"Fried Spam." He stared at her as if challenging her to complain.

She wouldn't, not when it tasted this awesome. She took another bite. "Getting your kitchen Mac-Gyver on before ten o'clock. Impressive."

And when he grinned, a day's beard growth highlighting his square jaw, her insides melted like the yolk on her noodles.

Stop that.

Whether the order was for Ryan and his knee-weakening smile or for her piss-poor resolve, she didn't know.

The food being so good gave her an excuse not to talk. She finished and started in on the dishes.

Ryan joined her and stared out the window at the falling snow. He hadn't lied about his shirt smelling like cedar. The warm scent drifted into her nose and tugged at her, tempting her to run her hands along the soft fabric. Giving herself a shake, she scrubbed extra hard at the pot he'd used to make the soup.

Not easy to do with him four inches away and looking more delicious than the meal he'd just made. Sweatpants and flannel suited him, both hugging his muscled limbs.

She nudged him with an elbow. "You cooked. I'm cleaning." Preferably with some distance between them.

He picked up a tea towel. Concern flickered on his face. "Hopefully I can get out of here by tomorrow. I only have the weekend off."

"Tomorrow?" The pot slipped from her hands into the water with a splash. The droplets showered her front and her face. She groaned. "Ew." She caught herself. "The dirty water. Not you."

"That's a relief." His mouth quirked, and he brushed the dish towel across the dots of water on her chin and cheeks. "And as for your objection to tomorrow, visibility's not great," he explained. "Doesn't look like it's letting up anytime soon."

She plucked the towel from his hand and tried to

dry off her sweatshirt. A lost cause. Enough water had sprayed up to soak through. "So you're just going to stay another night." She pulled the wet material away from her torso and shook it a little.

"I'm not trying to make your life difficult, Stella."

"Yeah, you're way near the bottom of the complications being thrown my way right now," she said. The cabin was free of the job-related tsunami of garbage that had swamped earlier in the week. Though hiding out here did bring a semblance of peace, she knew it was just temporary. She'd have to go back and clean up the wreckage soon.

So why not fully enjoy yourself for a few hours? Scratch the itch, so to say?

Oh, wait, because it was a stupid, *stupid* idea.

And yet…

But was it even what he wanted?

Ask. Or just dive in.

He was staring out the window again, drying their cutlery with lazy movements.

"Ry?" After wiping her hands off on the sides of her sweatshirt, she separated the garment from the thin tank she wore underneath and pulled the hoodie over her head. Even with the air in the cabin fully warmed by the roaring fire, goose bumps still rose on her arms.

A muscle ticked in his jaw, but he kept his gaze fixed on the trees.

She slid a hand up along his stubble-roughened

cheek and turned his face toward her. "Put the towel down."

"We're not done cleaning up," he murmured, eyes a molten blue.

"If you're stuck here, there's no rush to finish," she said. She scooted in front of him, fitting her body between the small counter and his bulky frame.

"What are you doing, Bella?" His voice was a low growl.

This time, she didn't protest the endearment. "Just taking advantage of the resources available to me." She let her palm trail from his cheek, down the open neck of his shirt, one finger pausing at each of the buttons until she was almost at his waist.

He caught her wrist with one hand and stroked her lower lip with the thumb of the other. A single "ha" came out on a snort. "Taking advantage of *me*?"

She nipped at the digit still caressing her mouth. "Mmm-hmm."

"Not possible. I'm one hundred percent here for this."

He was? She cocked her head. "But you were so concerned about what everyone thought. And I can see why… I ran into Georgie Halloran—"

A soft kiss cut off her words, making her legs downright shaky.

"Who isn't here. No one is. No one knows I'm here except your grandfather and my undersheriff," he said.

She kissed him back, eliciting a deep groan. She

settled her palms on his chest, feeling his heart rate speed up. "Leaving a travel plan. So responsible."

"People can get into real trouble in the wilderness."

Yeah, she was getting a firsthand example of that. "Good thing we're not actually lost. And you're an outdoor expert."

"An expert? Yeah, right." A frown tugged at his mouth. His hands tightened on her hips, holding her away from his body.

Damn it. She didn't want that physical space anymore. Emotionally, though, they could never close the gulf—there was too much between them. Things she hadn't told him; things he'd claimed not to want to know.

Should she be frank with him? Before they went any further?

Maybe...

But what if she told him everything about her pregnancy and miscarriage...and he reacted poorly? Then they'd be stuck in this closet of a space, with no way out and a whole lot of anger and hurt to keep them company.

No, best to wait until he asked to spill all that. And for now, she could use him as a distraction instead of futilely trying to distract herself from wanting him.

"When it comes to you, I'm no expert. I'm as green as they come," he continued. "I feel like I know everything and nothing about you, simultaneously.

And that this is both the best and worst path for us to explore."

"Like you said, there's no one here." She tilted her head to kiss his jaw, his neck. She felt his shiver under her palms.

"That is true…" He traced a line along her cheek before cupping the back of her neck.

Crack.

The sharp report came from outside.

"What was—?"

"A branch," he answered, posture shifting to protective. He pulled her against his chest and peered out the window. "Maybe a small—"

Crack.

Louder. Closer.

Ryan stiffened and swore loudly, shoving her down to the floor and crouching over her right before a cacophony rent the air and the ground shook.

Chapter Twelve

An hour later, Ryan's heart was still racing. He'd see that tree toppling to the ground in his nightmares for weeks to come. *There but for the grace of physics go I.* The angle had been a fraction off. The trunk had landed five feet from the cabin.

"Don't get me wrong," he muttered to the ten-inch fir, ducking his head to avoid the still-falling snow. He had a long afternoon of limbing and bucking up the trunk ahead of him. "I'm mighty glad you didn't land on me. But I'm a little choked you landed on my sled."

On the lean-to covering both snowmobiles, to be precise. Hell, he could be wrong about the damage. Stranger things had happened. But that crash had been more than the cracks of tree branches and the angled tin roof. It had sounded a whole lot like thousands of dollars of snowmobile repairs.

The methodical work—shearing off the branches for Stella to haul away, followed by sawing off foot-long chunks of trunk, piece by piece—at least kept his hands busy and off Stella's body. If a tree falling feet from the cabin wasn't a sign that they shouldn't be getting frisky, he didn't know what was. *Nah. Getting stuck here for longer? More like a sign that sharing body heat tonight is an excellent idea.*

Hopefully, they'd get back to where they were when they got interrupted. But first, they still had a hell of a lot more work to do. It was sweaty, silent labor. His stomach was growling and snow had made its way into far too many seams of his clothing by the time he finished with the chainsaw.

Stella had the branches in one pile and the wood stacked up against one of the cabin walls. Her cheeks were a beautiful rosy color. No different from the color they would have turned had they ended up having post-breakfast sex…

He stacked his hands on his head and groaned.

Thankfully, she seemed to misinterpret his distress. Arms akimbo, she scrutinized the heavily dented lean-to roof. "We're not going to like what we see when we lift that, are we?"

He shook his head.

"Well, let's get it over with." She stood at one corner of the roof and waited for him to take the other.

They hoisted the heavy panel. A mess of metal and plastic greeted them. The machines underneath were just as cracked as the tin and wood of the shelter, if not more so.

Stella swore.

He followed suit. "Goddamn it," he muttered, glancing her way. Her eyes looked extra blue, wide under the brim of her teal, cable-knit hat. She bit her lip, brow furrowed in silent question.

He motioned for her to set down her side of the roof. "No point in fussing with those—we'll have to haul them out with someone else's machine."

"Oh, dear."

"It's not the end of the world," he said. "Pain in the ass, sure, but Maggie and I both have insurance for our snowmobiles."

She seemed less than comforted. "But we're stuck here."

"For tonight, yeah. No point in having people come out in the dark to get us."

"You did."

"I was highly motivated." He winked.

Her lips thinned. "My grandpa left me his satellite-phone thingy. But isn't it for emergencies only? Can we just call for a pickup, or do we have to make a formal call to search-and-rescue?"

Ryan winced. He'd never hear the end of this from his department and the search-and-rescue crew. And so much for people not knowing he was out here alone with Stella. His hopes for privacy crashed to the ground harder than that damn tree had. "It's not an emergency. And it's easy to use them for texting."

Her mouth formed a moue. She was still wide-eyed. Still unconvinced.

"Come on. Let's clean up and get warm. We can fix this. Promise." Whatever it took to get her to believe he had things under control, he'd do it.

Fifteen minutes later, he stood next to Stella in the kitchen, waiting for the kettle to boil. Darn good thing there was so much snow outside—it saved them from having to use their drinking water to wash up.

Toes tapping, she clutched a plastic dish basin. "This place really needs shower facilities."

"Fishing's not fishing unless you actually smell like the fish," he joked.

"Except we weren't fishing. But I still smell." She plucked at her shirt, nose wrinkled.

"City girl."

She served him some solid "how is that news?" face. "A *million* percent."

He leaned closer, nuzzling the top of her head. "You smell like fresh air."

Scurrying backward with a squeak, she swatted at him. "Liar."

"Nope. I wouldn't lie to you, Stella. Not even about something surface-level."

Her lips parted, and something close to fear flitted in her gaze.

Hmm. He'd have to do something about that.

The kettle whistled. Ryan poured half in her basin,

and half in the one he'd set out for himself on the counter, and then stuck a snow cube in each to cool it down so it wouldn't burn. "Help yourself to the bedroom to get cleaned up. Holler and I'll make sure I'm decent before you come back out. Though you've already seen it all."

Her cheeks reddened past their already outdoor-healthy pink. "Years ago. And you've..." The slow scan down his torso left a trail as hot as if she'd traced that line with her tongue. She hurried off, disappearing into the bedroom without finishing the observation.

He couldn't stop the satisfaction from spreading across his face.

Gonna call for a rescue anytime soon? Or are you going to keep being lost in fantasyland where all that exists in the world is Stella and these four walls?

His conscience. What a buzzkill.

But a quick refresh and a change of clothes out-ranked contacting civilization. Who knew if Stella would be willing to pick up where they'd left off earlier? He sure hadn't gotten enough of kissing her.

She seemed pretty shell-shocked after the tree incident. But if he figured out a way to help her relax, and that relaxing involved some more kissing, or maybe even coaxing her off the couch? He wouldn't say no.

No one would believe that Stella and he hadn't slept together, not after finding out they spent two nights alone in a secluded cabin. So what was the point in fighting it? And then once she was back in the Big Apple, he could double down on finding someone as committed to Sutter Creek as he was.

Once clean and back in his flannel shirt and sweatpants, Ryan stoked the fire and settled onto the couch.

Now for the fun part of the evening—getting razzed over his predicament. Sighing, he turned on his sat comm and opened the message section. He needed to choose their rescuer wisely, reduce the chance of gossip. And the logical person who would both want to protect Stella and had sharp-as-hell rescue training was Lachlan.

On a scale of one to "I'm-already-packed," how eager are you to come fetch your sister and me from the fishing cabin tomorrow? Ryan sent the message and waited.

It didn't take long for a reply. Things not going well?

Hmm. That didn't sound like surprise, so Lachlan clearly knew Ryan had spent the night. Tom must have mentioned something. Now that he thought about it, the veterinarian's request reeked of fairy-godmother-level tactical brilliance. He shook his head. For now, Lachlan didn't need to know the details. Never mind all that. I'll buy you a beer and fill you in later. Our sleds are busted, and we need a lift out.

While he waited for Lachlan to reply, he sent a message to his undersheriff, too, who confirmed all was well with the department. Busy, but under control. He breathed a sigh of relief.

"Are you decent?" Stella called from behind him.

"Yep," he replied as he scanned Lachlan's reply. Tomorrow morning?

He was about to type *sure*, when Stella flitted by. A whole lot of long, peach-toned skin filled his vision. A skimpy, puke-green towel saved her from infringing on public indecency bylaws. Nevertheless, his jaw went slack, and he couldn't look away for the life of him.

She caught him staring, and snatched a handful of garments out of a duffel bag in the corner next to the packed bookshelf. "Forgot my change of clothes."

"I do not mind, Bella."

She growled. "Stop it."

He did, dropping his gaze to the device in his hand. He wasn't going to flirt without permission. But, damn, did he want her to give the go-ahead. He could swear the taste of her berry-sweet lip gloss still lingered on his tongue.

Lachlan's request for a time confirmation still glowed on the screen. The morning would be logical. But maybe, just maybe, if Ryan stretched things out a little longer, he could keep building on the goodwill he'd been working on since he arrived. She'd softened over the course of the day. Cooking for her had helped. And their silent teamwork had been a surprising success. In no world would anything resembling long-term commitment work between them, but continuing to repair some of the damage? That might be possible, and it would happen easier in isolation.

Liar. It's not about fixing past hurts, it's about pleasure. Mainly making sure you both walk away having had your fair share.

Okay, that, too. Because the truth was? Things didn't feel finished with Stella. And the most obvious tension was the electric pull between them.

Don't rush. Midafternoon's fine, he replied to Lachlan, pressing Send before he could second-guess his decision.

But the next step wasn't simple. It wasn't something that another impromptu burst of meal creativity would fix. It would take opening up. Even so, jazzing up the salad she'd planned to make and creating some ambience couldn't hurt.

Sticking a candle in a wax-covered Chianti bottle on the window ledge, he set the table for two. By the time she finally emerged from the bedroom, covered from neck to toe in layers of thermal clothing, he had makeshift falafel frying in a pan and was quick pickling a cucumber and diced onion.

She frowned. "I keep thinking I'm ready to get back to civilization, and then you pull something delicious out of your back pocket."

Guilt panged in his chest. Okay, then. She might not be so impressed when her brother inevitably mentioned having offered to come earlier in the morning, and that Ryan had delayed their ride home.

"Did you get ahold of Lachlan?" she asked.

"Yes."

"And…" She made a "keep going" circle with her hand.

"And he'll be here tomorrow afternoon."

Her nose scrunched. "Not earlier?"

"No."

Trying to keep things light, coax her back out of her shell, he regaled her with stories of some of the sillier parts of his job while they ate. She asked polite questions, but stayed behind her wall.

"You're a tough customer, Stella Reid."

Expression puzzled, she put down her cutlery. "How so?"

"I can barely get you to laugh, let alone open up."

Her eyebrows drew together. "I tried to open up the night you gave me a ride home. You shut me down."

Confusion filled him. "When you were trying to tell me about your case? I didn't want you to violate your NDA."

"You thought I was talking about work?"

"I did, yeah." Crap, in misunderstanding, what had he stopped her from confiding? "If it's something else, have at 'er."

A slow hiss of air escaped her lips. "I don't understand. I thought you wanted to leave the past in the past. But now you're being all charming and emotionally accessible. How am I supposed to read it all? Where are you going with it?"

He sucked in a ragged breath. "Well, I'm still attracted to you."

"I got that impression." The corner of her mouth twitched. Almost a smile. She took another bite of falafel.

Admit something that matters.

"When we got arrested—"

Her fork landed on her plate with a clatter.

"I couldn't handle it, Stella. The shame of it—and of having influenced you like that—"

"I was a willing participant," she said quietly. "Egged you on, in fact."

He scoffed. "You'd never gotten into trouble like that. As if I wasn't the bad influence. I sure as hell felt like scum. And my grandmother—for all her flaws, I owe her my life. Not in the biological sense, but when it comes to finding meaning… She tore into the detachment like an avenging angel, lawyer in tow. She woke me right up. My father's self-destruction—I saw that I could go that way. But didn't have to. Nothing was set yet." And the hard years of ranch work and college correspondence courses finally brought him enough pride that he didn't need to go looking for approval in unhealthy ways.

She didn't reply, so he kept going. "I was lucky. My grandma talked my great-uncle down. A mischief conviction—it's something I've had to be public about, obviously means I've been on a shorter leash at times, but it's not an automatic no for law enforcement. Especially since I was barely eighteen."

"You covered for me," she murmured.

"I stand by it. You didn't deserve to be arrested."

"I was a *willing participant*," she stressed. "I had just as valid a reason to get up to no good as you did. Maybe more."

"What, you'd discovered a Sutter Creek marauder's map?" he joked, taking a sip of his drink.

"No, I was panicking and desperate to rebel." Her lower lip tensed. "I was pregnant."

She'd been *what*? He choked on the liquid, put a fist to his mouth to stop from spraying water on the table. Eyes watering, he croaked, "Say that again?"

"I think you heard," she whispered, staring at her lap.

"Stella." A million questions raced through his brain. He wanted to hold her, but she was closed off, folded in on herself. He shifted off his chair and crouched next to her, awkwardly slinging an arm around her shoulders.

She looked down at him, eyes wet and mouth pinched.

He cleared his throat. "Is that why you came to the ranch that day?"

"Yeah."

He swore. "I was trying to do right by you. Thought you didn't need me, were better off without me—"

"I wasn't."

Shaking, he settled on the floor, legs bent, clutching her hand to his cheek and trying to catch his breath. How could he not have been there for her? How could he not have clued in?

His chest clenched and he jammed his free hand into his hair, desperate to divert some of the doubt ripping through him. And she obviously hadn't gone through with it. No judgment—she'd done what she needed to do. He sure as hell wouldn't have encouraged her to keep it, not at the place he'd been in at the time. The last thing she'd needed at eighteen was to derail her entire life with a baby. Look at how well that had gone for his own parents. But he had to ask. "Did you terminate before you left for school?"

"No." Her chin dipped to her chest and she slid to the floor, curling up in the space between his legs. The weight of her against him eased some of the tension gripping his gut. She slid her hand up, cupping his jaw. "I didn't know what I was going to do. I wasn't ready to be a parent. But I miscarried a week or so after trying to tell you."

She buried her face in his shoulder. Body shuddering, she clung to him.

"I turned you away," he rasped, frustration and shame cascading down his limbs, pooling on the bare wood floor. "Even before you came out to the ranch. I ignored your phone messages. Deleted your emails."

"I noticed," she said, choking on the words.

Goddamn, no wonder she was hesitant to trust him. That kind of pain, the life-hollowing abandonment—it didn't go away. He had his parents to thank for his own scars, and knowing he'd caused a fraction of that anguish for Stella…

His eyes stung, and he wiped them with the back of his hand.

"Hey," she said, lifting her head and brushing her fingers on his cheek. "I wasn't sure you'd be upset."

"About your miscarriage? It's—it's sad, but I didn't live through it like you did. It's pretty intangible for me."

Her fingers caught a tear from the inner corner of his eye. She held it up for him to see. "This says otherwise."

He shook his head. "I'm fine. Just surprised."

Fine. As if. He'd failed her. Turned her away and forced her to deal with something so life-changing without support. So, yeah, he was a little choked up. The knot expanded in his throat, tightening until it strained the muscles. He'd known he had a lot to make up for. Had been working to redeem himself in the eyes of the town, protect them and earn their trust. But that would all feel unfinished if Stella wasn't one of the people he won back.

He didn't spend his life obsessing about his mom leaving or his dad dying. It was better to move forward. But that didn't mean the pain disappeared. And for Stella… He didn't know how to make up for his desertion. Whatever remnants of his crappy choices wallowed in her hidden places—if they never went away, if she never managed to find peace with their past, would he be able to live with that?

Ryan's tears threw Stella for a loop. She'd expected stoicism, or anger. But not the repressed guilt and frustration that was coming off him in waves. She chewed the inside of her cheek, trying to minimize the comfort of being in his arms. Part of her clamored to explore the questions marking his expression.

Marking her soul.

But she'd been ignoring the emotional-support vacuum inside her for her entire freaking life. Seemed pointless paying attention to it now. Or expecting that he could somehow fill that void.

He can't. But he can make you feel good. Instead of believing a fix existed for the unfixable, she'd focus on hands and lips, muscles and skin. All the parts of him that could distract in the most delicious way.

Kneeling between his legs, facing him, she cupped both sides of his face and kissed him.

He leaned in, taking long, drugging sips. His hands slowly played her sides like a piano, thumbs brushing up her ribs, almost reaching the tender skin of her breasts. She hadn't bothered with a bra or underwear after she cleaned up, and desire pooled in her belly at the secret knowledge.

Pulling his lips from hers, he stilled his exploration of her torso. "I thought the tree falling killed any chance of this."

"But then you got all emotional, and apparently a softhearted sheriff is my candy." *No, that's what you need to avoid.* "Physically, that is," she corrected.

Sadness flickered briefly in his eyes. "Right."

"I don't even know where I'll be in a couple of weeks, Ry, let alone be able to make a long-term commitment like the one you need."

"Of course."

She reached for the buttons on his shirt, making quick work of the placket. Miles of hard, hair-dusted pectorals were on display, just waiting to be licked.

"Short-term, though? One night?" she asked.

"Hard to argue with one night."

She leaned in, mouthing a trail along his neck. "We've both been trying to argue against this."

"For good reason. But as long as it ends when we leave here tomorrow, I don't feel like arguing anymore."

"Good." Need swirled low, settling between her legs. She wanted to erase the space between them. Steal a few sweet moments of being close to him again. She pushed the shirt off his shoulders and arms and then pressed a fingertip to the center of his chest. "Let's see what we've learned since we last did this."

"I have been *innocent*, doll," he teased.

"Liar. And there you go again with that corny nickname."

His smile faltered. "Crap, sorry. Not sure why that keeps slipping out. Gross man habit?"

"Must be. And I shouldn't like it, but I do. I'm reclaiming it." She ringed her fingers loosely around his wrists. The hair crinkled, rough against her palms. "And I'm claiming you. Lie back."

Grabbing his shirt and jamming it under his head, he gave her a slow and sexy smile. She crawled forward, straddling his hips. Soft over hard. Her pajama pants and his sweats left nothing to the imagination, and yet was still way, way too much of a barrier. Bracing her hands on his chest, she rocked from side to side, relishing how quickly his body made it clear he was okay with her taking charge.

Pupils flaring, he caught her by the chin with the *V* of his thumb and forefinger. "Damn, you're beautiful. I missed this view."

Warmth bloomed in her limbs, affection more than arousal. Argh. It was supposed to be the other way around. Tonight was for bodies, pleasure—not feelings. She leaned down and kissed him before he could say anything else that tugged at her heartstrings.

She might have been on top, but he still managed to lead. A heartbeat, a breath, and he was kissing her like he'd been stuck on a desert island for years. His hands roamed on her hips, then under her T-shirt and sweater. One roughened palm cupped a tender breast, rasped across her nipple. She arched into him, rolling her hips. Heat pulsed, a wave along her flesh. She moaned her approval.

"Stella…" He was riding the line between warning her and being playful. "Where's your bra, doll?"

"Not on me." She took his hand and slid it down her belly. Her sex pulsed, wanting more than the friction of their pants over his erection. "Look harder. See what else you find."

She planted her hands on either side of his head and nibbled his neck. Maybe that angle would be easier to—

His hand slid into her pants, stealing her focus. He cupped her, tracing the seam of her opening with the tip of his middle finger.

A whimper filled the cabin. Hers. But, wow, that was definitely—

He reached for her cheek and brought her face in front of his, kissing her, watching her with a sly, secretive smile.

And still he traced a teasing line, not going farther than her outer sex.

She squirmed against his hand. "Do you think I left off my panties because I wanted to go slow, Sheriff?"

"I think you wanted to tease me. And it's only fair to return the favor."

The floor dug into her knees and she shifted, closing her eyes, trying to get him to go deeper. "More. Please."

One fingertip delved oh-so-close to heaven.

"Look at me, Stella. I want to see what you look like now when you let go."

"I'm close."

He flicked, and she melted a little more. He tsked. "You're in a hurry, and that's a damn shame. If we only get to do this once, we're going to do it right."

She gyrated her hips, pinning his hand between their bodies. "We said one *night*, not *once*. Unless you can only—"

"Try again." His next flick bordered on a reprimand, tightening the knot of desperation at her core. "Let's define one night as *all* night."

"Oooh-kay," she replied.

He slid a finger into her passage, plying her flesh until she couldn't hold herself up anymore.

"We didn't figure this one out in high school," he said, his own need evident in the hitching cadence of his words.

"Shh. Too much talking." She'd wanted him so much back then. And now…he was right, this was more. Better. How would she come back from this being better? But nothing in the world would stop her from chasing what he promised with his fingers.

He stilled his sensuous strokes.

"What?" she gasped, bucking her hips in a command to continue.

Laying another scorching hot kiss on her, he withdrew his hand. When she protested, he hushed her. "We had enough messing around on the floor as kids. This time, we're finishing in the bedroom."

Chapter Thirteen

The mattress in the utilitarian bedroom was nothing to write home about. But having Stella naked and sprawled on the sheet, her fingers gripping his hair while he coaxed her toward oblivion with his mouth, was all that mattered. He had one night to enjoy her, and he wasn't going to waste a single minute. So long as she found her satisfaction, his was guaranteed.

His palms caressed her ass. He kissed her center, smiling to himself as she whimpered and fisted his hair tighter. He could do this every day for the rest of his life and be—

No. It could only be about the here and now. He'd keep it about her pleasure, no matter how much a big part of him wanted to run with the fantasy of having more than the moment.

Flicking her tight bud with his tongue, he curled a finger inside her wetness and pressed the spot he knew would make her squirm.

"Ryan."

Another flick. "Let go, doll."

Her hips lifted. "I know, but I can't—"

"Sure, you can." He licked, loving the salt and earth of her. "Trust me. I can get you there."

A suck, a nibble, a blessed moment of feeling her crest, and she dissolved in his hands.

He lifted his head and reveled in the proof that she'd relaxed enough to reach the pinnacle. Her flushed cheeks. Her satisfied smile. The arm drawn across her eyes, hand hanging limp, palm up on the pillow. He kissed her center one last time and rose on his knees. He was as hard as the tree that crashed through their snowmobiles.

Patience. Savor it.

Taking his length in hand, he stroked.

"Don't you dare. That's my job," she ordered, rising on her elbows.

"Oh, you think so?" he teased.

"You showed me your new tricks. It's just fair I show you mine."

He crawled up the bed, gave his mouth a quick wipe with the back of his hand and kissed the corner of her lips. "I don't need tricks, Stella."

Delving her fingers behind his ear, she tilted

her face to take his mouth with hers. "What *do* you need?"

He reached to the single nightstand, fumbling for the condom he'd grabbed from his bag on their hurried stumble to the bedroom. "Just you."

A careful hand, a determined look, and she rolled the protection on him.

"Well, you have me." She smiled, anticipation edged with yearning. "For a few hours, anyway."

The truth of that dimmed the hope swelling in his chest. Could sleeping together, even without promises of commitment, show her how good they could be? Because as much as he knew they had no future, he wanted her to see that. To see that he could be the kind of man who would treat her the way she deserved to be treated.

"I want to see you come again," he murmured.

Smirking, she slid a hand over his erection and guided him toward her. "Confident."

"Damn straight." He thrust home, earning a gasp. Being inside her heat…oh, man—perfection. And her muscles, hugging his length, drawing him close to his own release—

Hold it together. You have promises to keep.

Gritting his teeth, he sank into her, setting a rhythm that matched her ragged breaths. Pressure built low, pulling at him to bury his face in the pillow and himself fully in her. He resisted, coaxing out every last moan and gasp that he could before she bit her lip and dug her nails into his back. Her cry, the rhythmic pulse of her pleasure, the two of them being joined together—he gave in to the call to topple off the cliff.

Sparks and flames streaked through his body, burning away his doubts. Overcome with the goodness of having her soft curves under him, of finding the peak together, he struggled to stay on his forearms.

She kissed him softly. "You're shaking."

"I know. It was that good." And given it was their only chance, they'd have to aim for even better as soon as he could collect himself.

"Making the best out of what we've got," she whispered.

He breathed deeply, putting to memory the smell of her mixed with the scent of sex. It lined up, threads of the familiar twining with strands of the new. His gut clenched at the limitations, at how much he could see them creating more memories, if only their life paths could be woven like their pasts. But they weren't. Tomorrow, this would be over. He'd stick to his promise. And he'd have to be okay with that, even if his heart was clamoring for forever.

Stella woke up, finally warm. She didn't need a blazing fire when she had Ryan to snuggle into. And they had, all night. He'd been lying there on his back, a solid wall of man, and she'd nuzzled against his side as if she was another half of a sleepy mold.

And his chest was *right there*… She pressed her

lips to his bare skin. A little good-morning nibble. He was still sleeping, probably wouldn't even notice.

"I don't think it's still nighttime, doll."

"Oh, what, you're going to quote some *Romeo and Juliet* at me, now? Nightingale, lark, blah blah blah?"

He chuckled, and the low sound hummed against her lips as she dropped tiny kisses across his chest.

"I'm going to quote *you*—'one night.'"

She froze. Frick, he was right. If she started making exceptions now, she'd keep doing it. And neither of them needed that. They'd had their fun, and it was over, and they'd keep moving forward. Separately.

He scrubbed his hands over his face. His stubble promised that three more days of not shaving and hiding in the cabin would make him irresistible.

Three more days and you'd run out of condoms and would probably end up pregnant again.

She growled at her base instincts. Yeah, all that rugged masculinity did intoxicating things to her insides, but part of being a freaking adult was suppressing any craving that took her focus off what mattered.

Or maybe my perspective on what matters needs some serious adjusting.

His arms banded around her, the strength so damn obvious in his taut muscles. She sighed, burrowing into the warmth.

Which could be treacherous to her state of mind. Because comfort meant finding a safe space in each other. Those spaces where, once upon a teenage dream, love had dwelled.

It's okay. It doesn't feel the same. She didn't have that manic craving that she'd had when she was younger. It wasn't desperate, frantic.

He was too solid for that. Too steady. Last night, those hands had fulfilled every promise he'd made. A confidence of knowing himself and knowing what he could do.

She'd had that once, before her work disaster. But it was gone.

Maybe you could get it back through him.

She recoiled, scrambling out of the covers. The cold of the room shocked like a bucket of ice water, and she grasped for the spare blanket dangling off the end of the bed.

Getting back her confidence through someone else? Hell, no. This was why she didn't do connection.

Sleepy confusion tilted his mouth. "What?"

"I don't need a relationship to find myself."

His twisted expression deepened. "When did I say you did?"

"You didn't." *But I needed the reminder to figure out my crap without dragging someone else into it.*

"Good—I'd never want you to think I thought that way. Why do you think we fell apart before? Youth, sure. But we were also using each other to hide from our problems. It took seeing how much damage that urge in me could do for me to realize I had to walk away." Closing his eyes, he shook his head. His hair rumpled on the pillow, and she held herself back from reaching over and fixing it.

"Are you actually upset about a baby that never was?" she whispered.

He opened his eyes, and regret deepened his irises to a stormy blue, piercing her to her core. "No. I mean... There are a whole pile of what-ifs we could entertain, but more relevant? I abandoned you. I've been there, abandoned by a loved one. And I did it to someone else. And, sure, I was young. But the impact hasn't faded, not enough. And I don't know how to fix it, Stella. I don't know how to repair what I did."

You can't. Because the problem isn't you anymore. It's me.

Tightening the thick wool blanket around her body, she hitched a hip on the edge of the mattress. A troubled thought crossed her mind. "Is that what last night was? Restitution?"

His silence jarred her.

"Ryan? Were you trying to make up for the past?"

"No," he finally answered. He pulled an arm out from under the covers and propped his head on his hand, making his biceps flex. "I want to show you who I am now. A pride thing, I guess. But I can't even begin to make up for walking out on you."

His honesty wrapped tightly around her chest, and she struggled for a full breath. This was exactly the way for him to fix his mistakes—just acknowledge how the situation had been bigger than he'd realized at the time. And that he regretted it, would have handled it differently had he known.

An unsettled feeling swirled in her stomach. Was it that simple?

No, not simple. Recognizing and admitting flaws were both big freaking things. And if she didn't guard against it, accepting his regrets would push her far too close to realizing how much she wanted to accept *more* about him. She could look at his face for days, obviously. But less obvious—she wanted mornings like these, just the two of them. To walk down the street with him, holding his hand. See him in the heart of the community he loved.

And given that he hadn't always loved it, could she find that kind of love here, too? In Sutter Creek? *With him?*

Something deep in her soul scoffed, and it sounded a whole lot like her mother. Right. She couldn't find love here. Sutter Creek wasn't her plan. Getting back what she'd lost at work required her singular focus. She'd escaped the noise long enough; she had a reputation to salvage and a payout to secure. Having an SEC-funded nest egg would be necessary for the next few years, given she didn't anticipate having a job to return to at Holden Management, nor would it be easy to get hired elsewhere. Firms couldn't technically fire whistleblowers, but they usually managed to under different language. The minute she got back to civilization, she'd buy a plane ticket back to the city. Being Stella Reid, hedge-fund analyst, didn't mix with Ryan Rafferty, county sheriff. There were a million awesome things about him, but he needed an equal exchange. He deserved someone as open and honest and trusting as he was, and she wasn't any of those things anymore.

So—downplay what's happening. Make sure he knows you haven't changed your mind about anything. "I see who you are. You're a good guy, Ryan. And last night was a lot of fun."

His jaw slackened. It took him a few seconds to reply. *"Fun?"*

She shrugged. "Yeah. Lots." She stood, then made her way out to the living area, catching the whine of an approaching snowmobile.

Squinting through the kitchen window, she spotted a single rider on a fire-engine-red sled, zipping along the trail. She glanced down at her blanket attire. *Oh, crap.* She was in no way prepared to face her brother, even if he was coming to help them.

"Didn't you say Lachlan would be here in the afternoon?" she called to Ryan, rushing over to her bag to throw on clothes.

"Yeah, early afternoon—"

The engine noise cut off, and less than a minute later a key clicked in the lock. A gust of frigid air blew in, along with her brother.

"It's colder in here than it is out—" His gaze flicked from Stella, half-dressed, to her shirt from last night, discarded on the kitchen floor, to Ryan stumbling out of the bedroom in his boxers as he yanked a sweatshirt over his head. "*Oh*. The 'body heat' method. Fair enough."

Hot prickles rushed over Stella's skin. Who needed a stoked fire when embarrassment did the job? "We didn't..."

Ugh, what's the point? She started folding clothes and packing them into her backpack as quickly as possible. Time to put her new plan in place: get back to town, book a flight to New York and clean up her mess. But Lachlan's smirk was too much to take to let him win.

"We didn't," she repeated.

"Yeah, you did." Lachlan grinned. "I assumed with the sled issues and the isolation, you'd be tearing your hair out to leave. But I see. No wonder Ryan told me not to come out until the afternoon."

She froze. "What?"

"That's the message I got." Her brother shot her a confused look.

"Figured we didn't need to rush," Ryan grumbled.

"You knew I wanted to get out of here ASAP," she said. "I would have been packed up and ready to go had I known Lachlan would be coming early."

Lachlan shifted uncomfortably, and his snow gear rustled. "I'll go out and take a look at the damage while you two figure out what you want to do. We'll have to take two trips on the snowmobile."

She glared at Ryan, who winced.

I want to show you who I am now. As if.

The second the door banged shut, she laid into

him. "You lied. Why? Were you *planning* on getting into my pants last night? Because if it actually was about proving you've changed, your strategy sucked. Unless being the golden sheriff requires being heavy-handed and making unilateral decisions?"

He swore. "I'm not going to pretend I didn't send that message on purpose, Stella. But it wasn't with the intent of sleeping with you. I just wanted..."

She waited for him to finish, but he didn't. He sighed and busied himself with packing his small amount of gear.

"You wanted what?" she pressed.

"Nothing that matters now."

Anger flared up the back of her neck. "No way. You don't get to slough off like that, with a half-baked excuse and apology. You know how much honesty matters to me. My dad lied to my mom all the time and—" She closed her eyes and rocked from her crouching position to sitting on her ass on the cold wood floor. Overreact much? She and Ryan were the definition of a one-night stand. Her parents' screwed-up marriage and divorce had nothing to do with this. "Ignore that. You're right—none of this matters."

He crossed his arms and set his jaw, as if they were back on the side of the snowy road and he was handing her a ticket. Impossible to go back to that sense of naive anger, though.

Everything that had happened since he'd arrived at the cabin—hell, since she'd arrived in Sutter Creek—all mattered.

When she stepped on that plane to return to Manhattan, she'd be leaving part of herself behind again.

"Glad we agree," he said through clenched teeth. "It's better this way. And I tell you what—take your belongings out with you on your brother's sled. I'll clean up here, and he can come back and get me. I'll bring your cooler and water jugs and the garbage out then. That way you can be home as fast as possible."

She couldn't argue with that, so she stood and stalked toward the kitchen area to check for things she needed to bring back today. He stopped her with one big hand on her shoulder, a hot brand despite the wool of her sweater.

He bent his head to her ear. "I won't claim I was right about the message I sent your brother. But last night, did I once not listen to what you wanted?"

Jerking her gaze to his, she stuttered, "N-no."

"And have I ever, since you got here, treated you with the kind of disrespect your father laid on your mother?"

"Of course not."

"Or acted in any way that would suggest I'm the risk-taking asshole you used to date?"

She shook her head.

He released her shoulder. "Good. Because I can't control where you live or what you want out of life, Stella, but I intend to make damn sure that you know that if you did live in town, I'd be doing everything I could to make you happy. And that was the reason I told Lachlan to come later."

"You—" Her mouth was so dry, she almost choked on the word. She swallowed, then licked her lips. Neither worked. She still sounded like she'd been horseback riding in the desert when she continued. "Make me happy now. Starting with not throwing meaningless promises around."

"Meaningless. Right." Eyes wide, he backed up and shoved his feet into his boots and his arms into his jacket. "I'll leave you to pack. See you in town."

He tromped out of the cabin, his bootlaces dragging behind him. The door banged shut, leaving her alone once again.

Chapter Fourteen

It was pushing late afternoon by the time Lachlan dropped off Ryan at his truck in the skiers' overnight lot. The couple of hours of silence at the cabin while cleaning up, along with the hourlong ride home, had provided plenty of thinking time. The ride back had been squishy, given Lachlan was only a couple of inches shorter than Ryan, but complaining would've been tacky given the ferry service had taken up most of the afternoon.

Lachlan sat on his sled in the snowy parking lot by the tailgate of Ryan's pickup, sizing him up. He'd cut the engine, allowing them to hear the hum of the nearby ski lifts. "I should get back home—Marisol's off and we were supposed to have some family time."

Ryan winced. "Crap, sorry."

"Stella's family, too. And you did her a favor, so I was just returning it."

"Not sure your sister would call what I did a favor—not anymore." Yeah, his lie had been small, but dishonesty was dishonesty. He'd promised to put any trace of his old, corner-cutting youth behind him. And the fact he was so quick to manipulate when dealing with Stella was a bad habit he didn't want to get back into.

Even if it had gotten them one passionate night together.

But now that he and Stella had agreed to one-and-done, he had to set that aside and focus on figuring out the cattle theft and keeping the peace and looking toward the election.

All things that required checking in at the detachment, so after saying goodbye to Lachlan and stopping by Tom Reid's to pick up the dog, he went to the emergency-services building.

After clipping a leash on Puddle, he donned a baseball cap to cover his rumpled cabin hair and strode into the building.

A tall woman with killer legs stood at the reception desk next to Graydon Halloran. Not the legs that had been wrapped around him last night, but Emma's.

He pasted on a smile. "Two Hallorans for the price of one. Managed to dig out from under the snow, I take it?"

Gray, who was leaning sideways with one elbow on the high counter, nodded. He wasn't wearing his customary smirk.

Emma came over and kneeled next to Puddle, who immediately rolled onto her back and presented her belly. "Oh, were you *lonely* after being without your daddy for the weekend? So hard done by."

Ryan snorted. "She was with Tom Reid all weekend. Got spoiled far more than if she'd been with me." He noticed dark circles under Emma's eyes. "You okay, Em? Snow keep you up?"

Her expression darkened and she stood.

Graydon straightened, his mouth flat. "We were up with Mom last night. Appears thieves used the blizzard as cover. We lost stock in the west pasture."

"What?" Ryan's sheriff mode kicked in. His brain started running possibilities, including a major one—why hadn't the undersheriff notified him via sat comm? Anger ripped up his spine, along with a good deal of shame for being unavailable during a crisis. "Excuse me. I need to go get caught up." He glanced down at his dog. "Damn it. I don't want to waste time by taking Puddle home, but I can't leave her in my truck."

"Give me your house key. I'll let her in for you," Emma said, holding her hand out for the leash.

An hour later he was out at RG Ranch, examining the makeshift fence that had replaced the one the thieves had compromised.

"The snow erased all tracks?" he asked his undersheriff, Nathaniel Wilson, who'd attended the call and managed the investigation this morning.

The rich brown skin of Nate's forehead wrinkled. "Anything useful."

"Damn it," Ryan grumbled. "I should have been here."

Georgie Halloran lifted an eyebrow, stuffing her hands in the pockets of her shearling coat. "We all missed it, Ryan. Even with regular patrols."

"You've changed your tune about my level of dedication to my job," he said before he could stop himself.

She drew back. "Feel free to take days off, Sheriff. It was who you were with that worries me, not that you were out of range for a night."

"Two nights," Nate corrected.

Ryan sent a "thanks for nothing" look at his second-in-command before softening his gaze for Georgie's sake. Nate snorted and strolled off, examining a different fence section.

"Stella and I are on the same page," Ryan said to the older woman. "Both of us have too much going on at work to even consider a long-distance relationship." It would be stupid to essentially pack his heart in her suitcase when she left the state. He'd done that once—his fault. And this time would be no different. If he got attached in any way, it was on him.

"It's not a long-distance relationship that worries me," she confessed.

Good grief. She'd really dug her nails into the

impossible, hadn't she? "Let's focus on the task at hand."

Weariness pulled at Georgie's mouth. "I dunno, Sheriff. If we keep getting hit like this, Rich and I might need to look at other options."

Fear stirred in his belly. "For where you put your support in the upcoming campaign?"

"Not exactly. For what we do with the ranch."

A gust of wind struck him, driving home her uncertainty. "Georgie, we'll track trucks at the highway stops, send alerts to slaughterhouses—"

Her shoulders slumped. "They're already gone, Sheriff. We both know that."

He did. If they managed to recover fifteen percent of stolen cattle in any given year, they were above average.

So work harder.

He put a hand on her shoulder. "Give me a few days."

Good thing he didn't need to spend time thinking about Stella. He'd be lucky if he slept this week, let alone worry about the woman who had thrown him for a loop. Again.

Don't book a ticket home yet. If you want to be eligible for an SEC payout, you need to make sure you don't put yourself in a situation where you'd break your NDA.

Stella sat in her sister's kitchen, staring at the email from her lawyer. What the hell? Wait *longer*? No.

It was too late on the East Coast to call, but she could at least email back.

What? How does informing the authorities and wearing a wire to work for months not prove that I'd keep my mouth shut if I was back at the office?

Her hands shook with impatience. Damn it. She had not expected to come back from the cabin to yet another holding pattern.

Her phone dinged and an envelope icon appeared.

These things don't move fast. Hoyt's bail hearing is in the morning. Gill still thinks distance is best. Let's see what happens before you make plans.

Before she *made* plans? She already *had* plans. Maintain some level of control in how she left her firm and start networking. And she couldn't do that stuck in Montana.

Stomping to the guest room, she frantically scanned the space for something—anything—to do. Her unpacked duffel caught her eye. Sad day when laundry seemed like a lifesaver. She dug through her bag, tossing her dirty clothes into the basket in the corner of the guest room. The yellow bra she'd worn yesterday landed on top of the fuchsia panties she *hadn't* put on after cleaning up post–tree removal, an eye-searing reminder of her bad decisions. She pulled out one last article. A shirt. Ryan's. Irritation prickled her chest. How had it gotten mixed in with her clothes?

Because you stripped each other naked so quickly that you didn't pay attention to what was going where? And this morning your freaking brother interrupted, and you packed with the attention level of a toddler?

Her stomach wobbled and she forced herself not to bring the shirt to her nose to inhale his sexy, masculine scent. If she kept the stupid thing lying around, she'd probably get all weak and end up sleeping in it.

Grrr.

Better to return it than fall into sappy habits like that.

Ten minutes later, she knocked on his front door.

It swung open, but there was no grumpy sheriff in sight.

Emma Halloran stood in the doorway, holding Puddle by the collar and wearing a suspicious expression. "Stella, hey."

Wow. He'd come straight home to Emma? What the actual garbage was that? Stella's heart fell to the stoop. She swore she heard it roll off the edge and land in the winter-denuded hydrangea. The empty pain of betrayal seared her to her core. Her eyes stung and she swallowed hard. He'd said he wasn't interested in Emma. And he might not owe Stella anything, but maybe a little courtesy would be nice, like let a freaking week pass before he invited another woman into his bed.

She lifted her chin and held out the T-shirt, extending her other hand to the dog, who was wiggling around Emma's perfect legs like an out-of-control ride at the summer fair. The gesture earned her a lick. All she really wanted was to bury her face in the Labrador's neck and sob, but no way was she going to show weakness in front of this woman. Nor did she want to see Ryan's face if he was home.

"This got tangled up with my things at the cabin," she explained. "If you can give it to Ryan…"

Emma shrugged and backed up. "Come on in and put it where you like. I'm just here dropping off the dog. When he found out that livestock were stolen from my parents' place last night, he took off like a bat out of hell."

Oh. *Jump to conclusions much?* Guilt swooped in, almost as quickly as the feeling of betrayal had.

Stella's arm fell to her side. "Your reasons for being in Ryan's house are none of my business."

Emma made an "I don't believe you" face.

"And you're just going to let me in? I thought your mom had me pegged as a criminal," she said.

Emma rolled her eyes. "Yeah, my mom. Not me. And Ryan just spent the weekend with you, and clothing removal was involved, so…"

Entering the main room, Stella folded the shirt neatly and laid it on the nearest surface—the back of the couch that divided the space into a living area and the dining room. "Just because I'm in possession of his shirt doesn't mean I was the one who removed it. Or that I was even around when it was removed," she said, turning to leave.

Oh, God, Stella, just stop talking.

"You're as much of a liar as your sister," Emma said, a laugh in her tone.

Stella whirled to face her. "What? Some friend you are, insulting Maggie like—"

"About being in love," Emma chided. "Maggie's super loyal. And I bet you are, too. But I watched her pretend she didn't have a thing for Asher last fall. And you're wearing the same 'passing a kidney stone' look on your face."

"What?"

"I'll be honest with you—if Ryan were interested in me, I'd be there in a second. But his heart's not up for the taking. I can't fight with that."

Good. She hated the idea of Ryan being with anyone else. Which was awful, because Emma seemed to be a truly nice person, and Ryan deserved to find love with someone…

But I wish it could be me.

"I'm not in love with Ryan." Stomach twisting, Stella took a step back. "Seriously. Go for it." She almost choked on the words.

Emma's gaze flicked to the T-shirt. Her mouth turned down. "Go for it? You don't mean that."

"I have to."

"Why?"

Stella stepped into the foyer. "I'm only here temporarily. And I think his grandmother—along with a good chunk of his voting base—would have a stroke if he and I had a fling. I don't want to screw up his election chances."

"There are opportunities to work in finance in Montana. Not exactly what you've been doing, but if you have an MBA, you have options."

"Again, that criminal thing."

Emma waved a hand. "You don't think that will blow over?"

"I honestly don't know."

"I bet my uncle would love some new blood to work on project management for the mountain."

"AlpinePeaks?" Stella knew it by reputation—it was well-respected and known for growth. But it didn't carry the prestige of working on Wall Street. That had been her target for so long. To give it up, to quit? Humiliating. "I'm not a project manager—"

Ugh, why was she talking to this woman about career prospects? Puddle rubbed up against her leg, begging for affection. She threaded her fingers into the dog's thick fur and took a breath. "Thanks for letting me in. I'd better go."

The last thing she wanted was for Ryan to get home and have to pretend that they hadn't spent all of last night naked. She left, resting her head on her steering wheel as soon as she got inside her rental car.

She'd maximize her last few days in Sutter Creek

with her family—who knew when she'd be able to get back if she was reestablishing herself at the firm, or potentially a new workplace?

From Monday to Thursday, she managed to follow through. She spent time with Laura, hung out with Maggie, got to know her half siblings' significant others better. Checked off every sister to-do box. Even managed to avoid Ryan all week—apparently, he was living and breathing the cattle-theft investigation. And when her lawyer called on Friday, saying that the CIO was close to accepting a plea bargain and asking her back for a Monday meeting with the investigators, she felt almost complete. Until Maggie walked into the kitchen right as Stella was booking her flight.

Her sister's face crumbled. "Can you at least stay for the final work party at the barn tomorrow?"

Stella couldn't say no to that. "Yeah. I can go back on Sunday." A thought crossed her mind. "You know, I'm not going to need all the money from the whistleblower settlement I'm hoping to get. You and Lachlan could start a full-on search-and-rescue-dog foundation, let alone a training facility."

Maggie shook her head. "Lachlan likes working *with* the animals. He doesn't want to be hung up in administration."

"Right. Well, it was just a thought." And it was a thought that bugged her all night long. Her brain pinged back and forth between how damn lonely her bed was, and the possibility of expanding on her half siblings' business plan. She dragged herself across the street to the barn the next morning, wearing her lone pair of jeans and yet another shirt she'd borrowed from Maggie—plaid flannel this time.

Okay. One more day of painting—one more day of dodging questions about Ryan—and she'd be on a plane back to normalcy.

This feels pretty normal, though. Coffee in a travel cup, bright January morning sun on her face. The yips of dogs from the kennel of Maggie's clinic, and the bangs of hammers filtering through the doors of the barn.

Shaking her head, she entered the facility. All traces of the fire were gone, and the place looked close to perfect. "Hey, Lach, Gramps, how—?"

Except it wasn't her brother or grandfather wielding the hammer. Ryan, biceps straining against the short sleeves of his black T-shirt, glanced over at her in midswing. The tool landed with a thunk, and he let out a yelp.

"Goddamn it!" He squeezed his eyes shut and fanned his hand rapidly, flexing his thumb.

"Crap, I startled you," she said, ignoring their audience—her family and the same crowd of search-and-rescue people as last time, plus Rafe Brooks and his son—as she rushed over and took his hand to examine it. The skin was split along one side. "You're cut. Sorry." She called over her shoulder for her brother. "Lach, where are the Band-Aids?"

"In the clinic. Over the sink in the staff room," Lachlan answered.

"Come on." She tugged on Ryan's wrist, avoiding connecting with that serious blue gaze.

"It's nothing, Stella. I'm barely bleeding."

"It could get dirt in it." She tugged again.

Sighing, he followed, clearly humoring her.

She pulled him along the short path between the barn and the clinic.

"Stella, you can let go. *Should* let go," he said quietly.

Of course. Oops. She dropped his wrist. "Sorry. Again. About that, too." She held the clinic's back door open for him and tried to ignore his sculpted pecs as he climbed the two-stair stoop. But that chest… So yummy. And it looked like he still hadn't shaved since the cabin. His stubble was veering into beard territory.

Need pooled between her legs, and she shifted uncomfortably.

He glanced back, tilting his head in question. "Coming?"

"No!"

He snorted.

Cheeks bursting with heat, she waved him forward. "I mean, yeah, I'm coming *behind you*."

"No way, Stella. You'd always come first."

God, she had to be the color of a tomato by now.

He paused and cupped her cheek. "And not just in bed. You know that, right?"

"Okay, now who needs to let go?" She skirted around him, passing the treatment rooms, and entered the staff room. The space used to be the house's kitchen, and the appliances and faded linoleum betrayed the original age of the building. "Maybe I'll buy Maggie and Lachlan a non-harvest-gold stove next Christmas." She made her way over to the cabinet and pulled out a red canvas first-aid kit with shaking hands.

Ryan rinsed his thumb in the sink and dried it on a paper towel before leaning a hip on the counter beside her. "Hey. Bleeding's already stopped. Don't worry about it."

She jerked her gaze to his. "I thought you'd be working your case today."

His forehead wrinkled. "We made some headway yesterday. Recovered one of the Hallorans's animals in a barn outside Billings. Made an arrest, which could lead to more. I figured I deserved a day off."

"Not much of a day off. Big news like that—you should be celebrating."

He grimaced. "Tried to go out with some work folks last night."

"But?"

"I wanted to see you," he grumbled.

She inched closer to him and palmed the center of his chest. So warm. And hard. She splayed her fingers. "You knew where I was."

"And we agreed to keep our distance." He smiled

wryly. "Amazing I managed to focus enough to do my job this week, knowing you were still close."

"You did your job well, no less."

"Took effort, though." He dipped his head and pressed a soft kiss by her earlobe. "I hear you're leaving tomorrow."

The disappointment knitted into those words snagged her chest. "Flying out in the morning. Meeting with the investigators on Monday."

One strong arm slung around her. She wished she could take that with her, feel that unyielding support as she sat across a conference table to give yet another statement.

"I'm sorry again for lying the other day," he said. "I'm mad at myself about that."

Spreading her fingers along both sides of his jaw, she reveled in the week's worth of sexy facial hair. "Of all the ways we've hurt each other over the years, I think we can let that one go."

He dropped his forehead to the crown of her head and she held in a whimper. Being close to him—it was the best and worst way to spend some of her last hours in Sutter Creek. She wanted to bottle his smell and take it back to New York with her. Spread it on her sheets so when she woke up in the morning, she could pretend he'd slept next to her all night long and was waiting for her in the kitchen with a cup of coffee and a devastating smile.

"I meant it when I said I wanted to show you how

much I've changed," he explained. "Failed there, I guess."

No way could she leave tomorrow having him think he was anything less than amazing. "Ry." She hoisted herself backward onto the counter so they were eye-to-eye. Taking his hands, she pulled him between her legs. He looped his arms around her middle, holding her right close. She kissed his temple. "You don't need to prove yourself to me. I see who you are. I see how I could—" Oh, God. She was not saying those words. Not even hypothetically.

He groaned. The hand at her waist sneaked under her loose shirttail. A rough thumb stroked along her belly. Need shimmered in its wake, a skin-on-skin vow of all the good things this man could give her.

"What could you see, Stella?" His voice was so low, so gruff, that she could barely hear it.

An honest response hovered on her tongue. Maybe by hiding her feelings, she had it all wrong. It wasn't like he hadn't already guessed what she was going to say. "I could love you again."

His eyes slid shut. Pain marred his features. "But you can't."

"Not without losing everything I've built."

"Stella."

Her pulse thrummed. She'd be hearing him rasp out her name in her dreams for the rest of her god-forsaken life.

And what kind of life is it going to be if I'm alone?

Shoving aside the question, she tried to kiss him.

He tilted his face, avoiding her lips. "I *do* love you, doll."

An unintelligible squeak escaped her throat. She'd waited eighteen years to hear him say that again, and it was as wonderful and terrible as she'd imagined. Her pulse raced. "I—"

"Don't," he said.

"But..."

"This'll hurt less if you don't say anything."

She buried her face in the crook of his neck. "Less isn't good enough. We shouldn't have let things get this far."

Two hands slid down her back, cupping her ass. "So let's figure out a way not to get hurt."

But that meant changing everything. All her plans.

Fear flooded her, stiffening her muscles and filling her mouth with a metallic tang.

"You're scared," he stated.

"You figure?"

"I am, too. You rolled into town, back into my life. Into my heart. And I've got a massive case to manage, and a campaign to plan. But I think it's worth exploring if I can do those things and love you. Doesn't anything good in life have some fear attached to it?"

"Well, yeah. But everything you mentioned requires me to live here."

He looked thoughtful. "There is that."

"But I have a plane ticket. And an ongoing investigation. And a career to rebuild." It was all she'd ever had.

"And a life to live," he said quietly. He tipped up her chin with his fingers and claimed her mouth in a long, bruising kiss.

And she melted all over him. Crossing her legs around his hips, she gave in to the craving she'd been repressing for a week.

"Only you feel like this," she said, her voice a half moan.

He lifted her off the counter and carried her over to the door, which he locked.

"I'm going to end up naked on the couch, aren't I?" she asked.

He kissed her neck, mouthing a slow trail up to her jaw. "If you want to."

"We weren't going to do this again." She tipped back her head, exposing more for him to nibble on.

He eased onto the love seat, taking her with him. Their limbs spilled over the edge. Flicking open the buttons on her shirt, he followed the path with his tongue. She writhed under his big, hard body, trying to coax him to kiss her breasts.

"Use your words, Stella," he teased, cupping a tender globe and sucking the tip.

Pleasure rocketed through her. "Mmm."

His hand shifted, unbuttoning her jeans. "Not sure I'd call that a word."

"Your hand. In. My pants." She arched her hips. "That's five."

Pupils flaring, he grinned. "Like this?" One finger trailed a hot line along her pelvic bone.

"We should be quick." She fumbled with his belt buckle and undid his jeans, pushing them toward his hips, along with his underwear. He was long and thick, and she knew if she could just get her own pants down, he could be inside her and all would be right with the world, at least for one short moment.

Or, knowing Ryan, not short. He'd sure as hell proved his stamina last weekend.

Grinding against his hand, she wriggled her own jeans low, spreading her knees and cradling his hips. His fingers were pinned between them, still coaxing, building her toward the release she desperately needed. Just one more. Tide her over for a while. *Forever.* "Condom?"

"Back pocket."

She snatched the packet with two fingers and sheathed him.

"This is *really* quick, doll. You sure you don't want to—"

Grasping his erection, she slicked her hand down his length, mimicking exactly what she wanted from him. "Ryan, please."

"Anything."

"Just you. Just… I need to let go. To feel you—"

He thrust into her, filling her, a sensuous, teasing stroke. "Better?"

"Yes. *No.* Why can't it be—?"

Setting a rhythm that she'd be dreaming about for

years, he slowly drove her toward the brink. She was need and pleasure, full and satisfied but wanting… The raw power of his body, the soft parts of his soul that he let her see—

Why couldn't she hang on to him? Make it work?

She dug her fingers into his shoulders and reached for completion, for the stars hanging just out of reach.

He kissed her softly. "I love you."

And she shattered. Clinging to him, she let out a sob. Tears pricked her eyes and she hid her face against his shoulder as she drifted back to earth.

Thank God she was leaving. Because he was so much. More than a quickie on an ancient sofa. More than their mingled, gasping breaths. He needed to hear "I love you," too. Deserved it. And until she could figure out how to say it, it was only fair that she board that plane and never look back.

Chapter Fifteen

Ryan held Stella tight as he sat on the couch, waiting for his body to descend from the pinnacle of pleasure she had sent him to. Had he been given a choice, he wouldn't have picked the Reid clinic staff room for their final intimate moment.

Intimate moment. That's underplaying it.

She blew his mind. And had him thinking about solutions, impossible choices. If he was going to hang on to both her and his heart, he might have to start making some sacrifices.

"I love you," he murmured, kissing the soft skin by her earlobe.

She jolted and leaped out of his embrace, leaving a hollowed, physical ache in her absence. *That empty feeling? That's going to be the rest of your life if you don't figure something out.*

"I— Ryan, I want… I don't know how…" She fussed with her shirt and jeans, fingers fumbling with her buttons. "We should go back to the barn separately."

"Why?" His brain stuttered in time with her clumsy attempts to get her clothes put to rights.

"The court of public opinion can't seem to decide if I'm the hero or a secret villain in a fraud investigation. You don't need that in your life."

"But I need *you*." His chest ached. How were they going to work this? "I'll take you how I can get you, Stella."

Her shoulders slumped, and she crossed her arms. "I'll—I'll have to think about it."

"So will I, but can we at least agree to keeping the conversation open?"

"Yeah. Okay," she said.

"And none of this 'leaving separately' BS." After rising and fixing his own clothes, he settled a hand at her lower back and guided her toward the door.

He expected her to shrug off the gesture, especially when they reentered the training facility, but she didn't. The small measure of acceptance warmed him to his core.

The high, arched ceiling had been fixed by the contractor before the work bee, and the room smelled of the wood used for the rafters and crossbeams. But he still had the scent of Stella's skin in his nose. He smiled to himself, loving the secret moments they'd shared even if things would be a mess going forward.

The work crew was spread out in the various rooms: the conference and teaching areas, storage spaces, the large training ring and Lachlan's office. A few pairs of eyebrows rose in their direction as they reentered. His buddy Rafe downright glowered.

Ryan sent his friend a cautionary look. Just because Rafe had been jerked around by his ex-wife didn't mean it was fair to lump Stella into the "manipulative ex" category.

He leaned down to Stella's ear. "Too bad they ripped out the loft. We had good times up there. Could have revisited it."

"With one hundred percent better use of contraception," she whispered. "We conceived a baby up there."

He startled. He still wasn't used to that yet.

His brain ran with the idea. The mental picture of Stella, pregnant with their child—but a year or two from now, not at eighteen—was pretty damn irresistible.

Reminding himself that was putting the cart on an entirely different road from the horse, he gave her shoulder a stroke and asked, "Where should we get started?"

The door opened behind them, and they both glanced back. A chattering crowd entered, a whole pack of Hallorans. Emma, Graydon and Nora, the oldest. And Georgie.

Georgie frowned, matching Rafe's earlier dark expression.

Yikes.

She wiped her feet on the brand-spanking-new doormat, as her kids dealt Ryan various looks of sympathy and spilled into the room.

Stella looked up at Ryan, clearly concerned. He kept his hand exactly where it belonged. He was done with hiding, with worrying about what the future would bring. He knew Stella was innocent, and if his supporters couldn't see that, that was on them. And if it impacted him? He'd deal with that when it came.

"I hear Ryan and his deputies arrested someone for last weekend's theft," Stella commented to Georgie. "You must be thrilled, given how hard it is to crack a livestock case."

Georgie's jaw was tight, but she nodded. "I am. And it's pretty important to me that he's able to keep doing what he does best. And if he's planning to up and move to New York…"

Stella lifted a hand, palm out. "Well, we're not—"

"If that's what it takes to keep Stella," he interrupted, shifting his palm from her back to her shoulder, "it's not out of the picture."

He loved Sutter Creek. But he loved Stella more.

Stella went rigid under his touch. Blue eyes pierced him, confusion and fear and her own measure of love mixing in their depths.

"Ryan," she said, the word almost a breath. Then she laughed, the sound tinny and hollow, and nudged him playfully with her elbow. "This guy, Georgie. I tell you. He's a real joker."

Georgie narrowed her eyes. "Since when?"

"Since now, apparently. But don't worry, I'm not going to let him give up what he has here anymore than I can walk away from what I have in Manhattan. We've both worked too hard to establish ourselves." Stella patted the hand he still had on her shoulder before shifting away from it.

He locked his knees to make sure he didn't fall over from the weight of her words.

"Stella—" It was all he could choke out.

"You're going to tarnish your reputation for nothing," she chided, her voice carrying a strange tinkling note. "And I'll be on a plane tomorrow."

Yeah, with his heart sitting in her lap as the aircraft ascended into the sky.

Georgie regarded Stella disdainfully. "You always were good at running."

Stella's jaw dropped, but she didn't defend herself.

And if she's not willing to fight to figure out a way around distance and complications, then this won't work.

If she actually loved him, she wouldn't have made a joke of him like she just had, no matter how scared she was. He'd put every part of himself out there, and she'd shot him down hard, her belittling words riddling him with holes.

Faking a laugh, and knowing it came out awkward as hell, he nodded at the two women and brushed his thumb along Stella's cheek one last time. He'd have to call Lachlan and apologize for cutting out early, but no way could he stick around.

"You know, speaking of that case, I should probably get over to the detachment and check on a couple of loose threads. I'll update you as soon as I can, Georgie. Stella—" he scanned her, taking in her tipped chin and flashing eyes one last time "—travel safe, now."

The door clicked behind Ryan, waking up Stella from her frozen state. Georgie's accusation—"you always were good at running"—had hit her square in the chest. Her mind had been spinning so hard, she'd lost every part of the "smooth-talking, sharp negotiator" reputation she'd carved out since college. And now Ryan had walked out, pain sparking in his blue eyes like ice fragments in the sun. She had to fix this before she left tomorrow.

Pinning Georgie with a firm stare, she said, "I don't know why you and Gertie think I'm out to tear Ryan's life apart or rip him away from the community he loves. I don't think that's best, either. He loves this place, loves protecting it and feeling a part of it, too much for me ever to want to ask him to give it up. But if that *was* what he wanted, you all should support him. Just like he has the rest of you for his entire career."

Georgie, eyes wide with shock, smoothed a hand

over her pulled-back hair and opened her mouth to speak.

Stella held up a hand, indicating she wasn't done. "As for the headlines about me, I can't discuss them with you. But Ryan trusts me, as does my family. Doesn't that count for something?" Before the older woman could reply, she added, "Excuse me. I need to go apologize to him."

Georgie nodded slowly. "Well, good luck then."

Stella looked to the ceiling in disbelief. "Right."

"No, I say that with all seriousness." Georgie held out her hand, a genuine gesture of goodwill.

Stella shook it, and then bolted out the door after Ryan. She tore around the clinic and saw him climbing into his truck across the parking lot. "Wait!"

He stilled, one foot on the running board, and watched her approach.

The air bit with a January frostiness that was only outdone by the chill in his expression.

"Forget something?" he asked, voice ragged.

She stopped a few feet away from him. Shivering, she shoved her hands into the pockets of Maggie's hooded sweatshirt. "Yeah, my mind, for a second. I'm sorry. Implying you weren't serious about your feelings—I shouldn't have said that. I know you mean it."

His knuckles tensed on the door of the truck. "Yeah, I *know* that you know. But you said it, anyway. Embarrassed me in front of the people who will influence whether or not I get reelected."

"I'm sorry." She reached to cover the hand he'd braced on the door of the truck with hers.

He pulled it away before she could make contact. "I accept that, I do. We all say stupid crap to protect ourselves now and again. But it doesn't change how you're still trying *to* protect yourself. If you can't trust me after I publicly announced I love you enough to *move*, there's nothing else I can do."

A lump filled her throat. She didn't resist it dissolving, didn't bother to hide the tears that spilled over her cheeks. "What if—?"

No. There was no use in asking for a second chance, for more time to find a solution. What was she thinking? Stella had only been good enough for her dad when she was getting professional accolades. She'd never been good enough for her mom. And Lachlan and Maggie—they loved her, despite the fact she didn't know how to properly love them back. And she saw how much that hurt them. So why do that to another person? Ryan was right—he deserved better than what she could give him.

He stared at her, clearly waiting for her to continue.

"Okay." She sniffled, wiping her eyes. "Yeah. You, uh, take care of yourself. Good luck with that case. Hopefully you're wildly successful and put all the bad guys in jail without it going to hell on you like it has happened to me when I tried to do the same thing."

"Stella. With that—" He swallowed, throat bobbing. He rubbed his jaw, his fingers grazing the short beard there that she hadn't gotten enough time with. "Call if you need help."

He climbed into his truck and drove off.

"He said *what*?" Gertie's knees shook and she sat on one of the benches in the town square, disbelief coursing through her veins. Was her hearing finally starting to go? Or maybe her cell phone needed replacing? Because Georgie Halloran couldn't be correct in her recounting of what sounded like Ryan having offered to move to New York and Stella having rejected him in front of the barn work crew an hour ago. "He can't— *Moving?* My God."

"I'm not sure if Stella managed to patch things up when she ran after him, but he looked mighty brokenhearted when he left the barn," Georgie informed her. "He said he was headed to work."

"Well, thank you for telling me."

Hanging up and pocketing her phone, she hurried over to the emergency-services building. The sheriff's department was dark and silent but for a small light and the clacking of a keyboard coming from Ryan's office.

"Honey?" she called, approaching the open door. She halted in the doorway. Ryan's mouth was turned down, as if he'd never be able to smile again. He didn't look at her. The cold, stony gaze that looked way too much like his father's stayed fixed to his computer screen.

"Sweetheart, I—"

"I want to be alone, Gran," he barked.

Alone? She seriously doubted that was what he actually wanted. Oh, dear. He'd fallen in love with Stella again, and she'd interfered just like Tom said, contributing to her grandson being miserable.

She took a step forward. "You shouldn't—"

"Please stop telling me what I should and shouldn't do. Seriously."

She lifted her chin. "That's fair. I'll—" What could she do but follow his request? "I'll leave you then."

"Join the crowd," he muttered.

"Oh—" She stopped herself this time. No. She needed to fix what she'd done. And pushing him while he was so devastated wasn't going to help with that.

Another man could help, though. The one person who might get through to the woman Ryan clearly loved.

It took her an hour, but she tracked down Tom Reid at the hardware store. He was examining a display of screws, nails and other fasteners.

"Screwed," she said. "Theme of the day."

Tom eyed her with interest and a measure of concern. "What's wrong, Gertie?"

She repeated what Georgie had told her, and the mood Ryan was in. "How's Stella?"

"Haven't seen her. Maggie told me that something had gone on at the barn, but I missed the action."

"We need to help them solve their problems, Thomas."

Tom chuckled and tapped the carpenter's square in his hand against his other palm. "That's what I've been trying to do all along, Gertie. You're the one who's been at cross-purposes."

Her cheeks went hot. "I've changed my mind."

"Why?"

She took a deep breath and let it out. "I'm not so set in my ways that I can't admit I'm wrong. And seeing my grandson hurting so badly... I can't take it. I've wanted him to feel rooted, to have a place. He never had that when he was younger, no matter how hard I tried. And he's come into it now. But I think..." She squeezed her eyes shut, her throat tightening and making it hard to finish.

Tom waited patiently. He took one of her hands and squeezed. And she didn't pull away. She hadn't held hands with anyone in over a decade—not with a man she found attractive, anyway. So innocent, unremarkable, and yet the thrill of it took her breath away.

She gathered her courage. "I think his place is with Stella. No matter where she is. The love they have now could be different than the one they shared in the past."

Tom screwed up his mouth in thought and appeared to take a steadying breath of his own. "Just like love between us wouldn't have to look like your marriage?"

Her mouth dropped open. Love? Nonsense.

Or a damn good idea.

"What do you mean, 'like my marriage'?" she asked, voice shaking.

He tightened his grip on her hand. "I mean I'm not looking for a wife to run my household, Gertrude. I know enough about you and Reg to know that your happiness wasn't his top priority. But that's not how I like to approach things. I want a companion to share adventures with. And the mundane, too. I'd love you, if you let me."

She put a hand to her mouth, unable to reply.

"Gertie Rafferty, speechless?" he teased. "I must be doing something right."

"Oh, you are," she said, almost gushing.

He tugged her a little closer. Her shoes squeaked on the linoleum as she came close enough to him to smell the laundry detergent on his shirt and his faint, masculine cologne. "I'll talk to Stella, provided she'll hear me out. But first, I want you to agree to that date."

"Dinner? Now? I—I'd love to." She glanced around, finally registering that he'd declared his love in the middle of the hardware store. "We'll be the talk of the town for days."

"The tables have turned, my dear."

The sweet nickname warmed her to her very center. Lordy, when was the last time *that* happened? "I think we should give them something more interesting to talk about, don't you?"

"Such as…"

"Oh, I don't know."

But she did.

Tilting her face to his, she slid a hand along his smooth cheek and pulled his lips to hers. He tasted of mint and promises, and the heat in his eyes and the smile he gave her once they broke apart hinted at more.

"Take me for dinner," she said. "And then we'll figure out how to make sure our grandchildren end up as happy as you just made me."

Chapter Sixteen

The sun had barely risen the next morning, and Stella was up, jamming clothes into her suitcase. No time for folding. She, Lach and Maggie were planning on talking next steps for the SAR dog school over breakfast, and then she'd be off to Bozeman to fly back home to New York.

But this is home.

The words echoed in her chest like she was standing in a deep crevice.

Was Sutter Creek home?

A knock sounded on the door. "Stella, love?"

"Come in, Gramps." She buried two pairs of shoes that had gone unused on her visit, because who wore heels in Sutter Creek when it was January and the main activities were drywalling and holing up in a cabin? She gave her grandfather a wobbly smile. "I need to finish packing before Maggie, Lach and I hash out what they need me to do next for the business."

Gramps huffed and sank on the edge of the bed, posture still military-straight. "Well, at least you're tying up some loose ends before you leave."

She shot him a warning look. "I've been their biggest supporter through all this."

"Financially," he said.

"That's what they needed!"

"Nothing wrong with being the banker *and* a sister, honey. You can do both. Just like you could balance your work and your love life."

She sighed. "You say that like it would be easy."

"Come now," he chided. "No one ever promised anything would be easy. You've never gone the easy route, and I'd never suggest that you do. But even when you're on the hard road—the one where the rewards are so damn worth it—there's more than one turn you can take. New York suited what you needed—adventure, challenge, to be seen—when you were fresh out of school. But is that still what you need?"

"I don't need to be barefoot and pregnant if that's what you mean. I narrowly avoided that."

He waved a hand. "That's not what I meant. Not that there would be anything wrong with you wanting a family."

"Now, no, but having a kid wasn't the right path for me at eighteen. And I still need all those things that I did when I was younger. Regardless of whether someone is a parent, who doesn't want adventures? And to be challenged? To *matter*?"

"Maybe you could find that elsewhere, though. Here, even."

She lifted an eyebrow as she stuffed her sweaters into her suitcase. "How? Apply to work at Alpine-Peaks, like Emma Halloran suggested? Anything I could do in Sutter Creek is miles from what I do now, Gramps."

Except for what I've already been doing through financing Lachlan's business...

He shrugged. "Something to consider, given how unhappy you were when you got here."

Her back prickled. "Not true. I mean… I'm not enjoying being ostracized by my colleagues. But the work didn't make me unhappy."

"Not making you unhappy sounds like a pretty crappy metric, Stella. There's filling your professional portfolio and filling your soul. And there's nothing wrong with some of that fulfillment coming from spending time with another person. Sharing love and moments and dreams." A secret smile crossed his face.

"What's that expression for?"

"Let's just say I convinced another woman to open up yesterday. And I'd really like to have a two-and-oh record this weekend by getting through to you, as well."

"Is that why you weren't around last night? You were off courting some lucky woman?" He looked so damn pleased with himself, and something panged in her chest. Jealousy? Nah.

Um, try again.

Fine, she was jealous of her grandfather.

And her sister with Asher, and Lachlan with Marisol. And if she was being totally honest with herself, yeah, part of her yearned for a little peanut like Laura…

His mouth quirked. "I figure if I keep Gertie busy, she'll leave you and Ryan alone."

Her jaw dropped. "You're *dating Gertie* to keep her out of my business?"

"No," he said, suddenly serious. "I'm dating Gertie because she's a hell of a woman and I enjoy her company."

The pang mushroomed into a full-on green monster. "I'm happy for you, Gramps. And I'm sorry to ruin your lucky relationship streak, but I don't see how I can find a compromise that doesn't hurt either Ryan or me."

He winked and strolled toward the door. "Day's not over yet. You could still come to your senses."

His advice nagged at her until the moment she sat down at the table in the clinic staff room, waiting for Maggie and Lachlan to arrive.

Ugh, why hadn't she asked for a location change?

Not twenty-four hours before, she'd been on the sofa in the corner, moaning Ryan's name and going wild under him. And it was absolutely impossible not to let herself get consumed by the memory, by wanting more of him every day of her life.

She busied herself making three lattes with the deluxe Italian espresso maker sitting on the counter. Stella hadn't noticed the fancy appliance yesterday. She'd been too busy hungrily cataloging every angle and plane of Ryan's body.

Footsteps approached, and a chair scraped at the table. Stella glanced back to see Maggie settling in at the round, thrift-store special. A stretchy, turquoise band held her hair off her face. She wore yoga pants, a thin hoodie with thumb holes and the smile of a woman who'd been woken up by a loving partner in the mood for mutual enjoyment.

I could have had that, too. But she couldn't let Ryan throw away his life here. He wouldn't be happy in New York. *She* wasn't happy in—

She shook off the thought. "Your furniture's at odds with your coffee maker, Mags," she commented, plunking a froth-topped drink in front of her sister.

"Some things are worth the investment," Maggie said casually.

But the comment smacked Stella across the face. It was too similar to her grandfather's observations to ignore.

She resisted another glance at the love seat, another slip back to Ryan's hands on her skin, playing her, pleasuring her.

Task at hand. She smoothed her cashmere sweater and sat at the table across from her sister.

Lachlan strolled in, carrying a paper bag with the Peak Beans logo on it. He pulled a stack of napkins from his cargo pants, then dropped a card-stock folder in front of Stella, put the bag on the table and unzipped his fleece jacket.

"For your perusal, financial oracle," he said. "Please tell me we're going to be okay. That the insurance money will cover what we need so that I can resume my programming and make enough to increase the scope of what we do here."

She scanned both the revised budget and the schedule Lachlan had made, encompassing the building completion and a proposed ramp-up of classes and programming. It was enough to keep him busy. Enough to keep three people busy.

And you're used to working two jobs' worth in a week.

"Lach, if you had more money, what would you do with it?"

He lifted a shoulder, then took the last latte off the counter and drank deeply. "Train more staff. Build larger kennels, provide more programming."

"No, Lach. Millions. What would you do with *millions*?"

He froze for a second, eyeing her with caution. "Buy the acreage behind us. Build a dormitory.

Lease a large chunk of Ned Franklin's back forty to expand the beginner and advanced training areas to beyond avalanche and wilderness searches. But, Stella, millions of dollars don't grow on trees."

"No, but they do come from the SEC when a whistleblower gets a percentage of the sanctions. If I get a payout, what would you think about growing your school into a foundation?"

Maggie's mug clattered on the table. "As if Lach doesn't have enough to do running the place?"

"I could help out. I've worked with enough people who are involved in running or supporting charities that I'd at least know where to go to ask."

Lach crossed his arms. "You're going to do that and work your job at the same time?"

Closing her eyes, she blurted, "I don't want it anymore."

She could have sworn she heard the hiss of a pressure valve releasing. The band that had been clamped around her chest since she first called the authorities snapped, letting her take a full gulp of air.

And with the lungful came a spill of honesty. "When I meet with my lawyers and the investigators tomorrow, I'm going to make it clear that even if the new firm leadership decides I'm not persona non grata, I have no interest in returning. And trying to rebuild trust in the industry—I could do it, but it sounds…" A week ago, she would have said "necessary." Or described it as a challenge she couldn't wait to take on. But she couldn't make herself do it anymore. "It sounds exhausting." Her palms went clammy and she wiped them on her black wool pants.

"And you want to run my school as a foundation," Lachlan mused.

"I know, it's a pie-in-the-sky idea. I mean, if I don't get the payout, that level of funding would be an impossibility. Unless I invested what I already have wisely, contact some people I know and fundraise… I might get the money in other ways?" She caught Maggie and Lachlan blinking at each other incredulously. Right. That sibling connection she'd never have. "Sorry. I'm foisting my own needs onto your business."

"*Stella.* How many times do I have to tell you? It's your business, too. And if you want to grow it past my own vision, I'm here for that," Lach said. "We're both here for *you.* Is anything—anyone—even close to that waiting for you in New York?"

"Of course not." A ball of fear spun in her belly. "But what if I try to create something here and it falls apart? Even if I'm doing the right thing? I did the right thing after I got my promotion, and everything collapsed on me! And if I'm here, and you guys are depending on me, and Ryan's depending on me, and that falls apart, and I've taken not just a bunch of unethical fraudsters with me, but the people I love?"

Maggie scooted her chair ninety degrees around the table and wrapped her arms around Stella. "Hey. It's easy to forget how to trust your gut. Getting screwed over will do that to a person. But you're principled and smart. You've kept our business alive and allowed Lachlan to take on something he's dreamed of doing forever. And we'd love to take risks with you. Grow his dream until it's yours, too. And we'll call you on things if we think you're making a mistake."

"Which you are, by the way," her brother interjected.

Stella stiffened and looked at Lachlan. "What do you mean? I thought you just said—"

"With Ryan," he said. "You think we can't see that you've fallen in love with him again? He'd give you the world if you let him."

"I can get myself the world, if I want it," she said, a knee-jerk defense.

"Sure," Maggie agreed, giving Stella one last squeeze before ending the hug. She kept her hand on Stella's shoulder. "But it's more fun with company."

She studied her hands. "You two are used to that. You've always had each other. Full siblings. That bond…" She cleared her suddenly clogged throat. "I've always been alone."

Maggie scoffed. "Enough of this full or half siblings crap. That's all in your head. It's not something either of us think about. Yeah, Lach and I are close. We work together and live near each other and drive each other nuts. It's great. And if you lived nearby, it would be the same with you."

Maybe… Maybe it would. Yeah, making connections involved risk. But she'd been dealing in financial risk her whole career. And the biggest payoffs came when the most was on the line. When she *had* listened to her gut. She'd been focusing so much on what doing the ethical thing had cost her, that she hadn't properly counted up what she'd gained.

Her home. Her family.

Ryan, if she could earn one more chance...

Maggie squeezed her shoulder. "That little voice in your head, the one that's telling you to stay? Listen to it."

Stella nodded, mind whirring. "I still have to go back. But I'll book a return flight as soon as I can. We have work to do." She groaned. "And groveling. I have so much groveling to do after Ryan laid himself out yesterday—"

"I'm sure he did," Lachlan quipped.

She smacked him upside the head. "Not like that. Emotionally. And he deserves the same back tenfold. Starting with me telling him I freaking love him." She paused, tension threatening to freeze her vocal cords.

She could wait until she got everything settled in New York...

No. She'd do it now. She'd waited half a lifetime—that was long enough.

Chapter Seventeen

Ryan had never been so thankful to have a Sunday shift to work. He responded to a call from Adelita Brooks, who was worried about an intruder in her backyard shed that turned out to be a family of raccoons, and then checked out a lead on the livestock thefts that came up empty. He didn't mind the lack of success as much as usual. Because he needed to do something, keep his hands busy, stop himself from dropping all his principles and pulling over Stella on her way to Bozeman.

He'd contemplated it—slowing her down enough to make her miss her flight. One last selfish, desperate attempt to get a few minutes with her to tell her he loved her and hope she finally returned the sentiment. But pulling her over without cause wasn't going to build trust. And yesterday had been mortifying enough without making a spectacle of himself on the job. He was going to have to let her leave, and hope to hell she got to New York and had a change of heart.

Ryan sighed. He could learn to live with his heart ripped from his chest, right? Out and bleeding for all the world to see?

He pulled his patrol truck around the back of Peak Beans on Main Street. He'd eat, but not at the bakery. He did not need the full-court family press.

He was standing at the counter, waiting for his sandwich and coffee, when a familiar voice jarred him.

"There you are!"

Spinning, he leaned his elbows back on the high counter and shot Gran a questioning look. She had Georgie Halloran on her heels, and both women wore sheepish smiles.

"Did you hide a tracker in my boots?" he grumbled.

Gran swatted him. "We've been looking for you all morning."

"That's not a no."

"We saw your truck," Georgie explained. "And you weren't at the bakery."

"You skipped church?" he said to Gran.

She lifted her chin. "I was worried about you."

He pressed the heel of his hand to his sternum. "Unnecessary."

"You're not having chest pains, are you?" Gran barked.

"I'm thirty-six," he grumbled.

"It's heartache." Georgie's smile turned sad. "And in my shortsightedness, I contributed to that."

"We both did," Gran said. "We were trying to protect you. Messed that up but good."

"Again, I'm thirty-six."

"Sweetheart," his grandmother chided. "You spend your whole life protecting other people. Sometimes, you need to accept it in return."

Ryan drew himself up. The barista handed him his order. He took the travel cup and bagged sandwich, then motioned for the women to retreat toward the front door. "Accept you getting in between me and the woman I love? Can't say I like your tactics," he snapped, unable to keep his turmoil to himself.

Was it really fair to blame Gran and Georgie, though? At the end of the day, it was about Stella not feeling confident enough to be with him. And he had to accept it wasn't anything he could fix. She'd been hurt as a kid, neglected by her father and shaped by her mother's bitterness. Achievements were her only security. That was something he couldn't change, beyond having said what he already had.

Gran appeared chastised. "We owe you an apology. Which is why we're here."

"Especially me," Georgie said. "Gertie at least

has the excuse of being family. All I can say for my-self is I'm stressed about the ranch, and I've shifted that on you."

"I'm working on fixing your troubles," he mur-mured, sipping his coffee. "I know it's a slow pro-cess but—"

"Not what I mean," Georgie interrupted. "You've been doing your job, Ryan. Better than the last five sheriffs we've had. But the fact the ranch is on the razor's edge of being in the red isn't your fault. Nor is the fact my heart's not in it anymore. I'm going to be making some changes, and I'm sorry it took interfering with your life to make me see that noth-ing external will make me feel good about the ranch anymore."

"Changes?" he asked.

"I've been tied to Sutter Creek for decades, put-ting off all sorts of adventures while trying to keep the ranch afloat. It's not working, and I need a new plan. Gray and Emma are too busy to be involved. Bea wants nothing to do with it. So it's only Nora. And I can't ask her to shoulder the load while her father and I go off on an adventure."

He had a feeling that was exactly what Nora would want, but he wasn't about to tell a mother that she misunderstood her daughter.

"Rafe might…" He didn't finish the suggestion. His friend had enough going on with his own prop-erty and family to absorb any of the RG Ranch prop-erty or livestock.

"Nora would disown me if I sold a bucket of used nails to Rafael Brooks, let alone part of our ranch," Georgie said, smiling wryly.

She opened the coffee-shop door and was about to exit when a blur of black wool and blond hair burst into the shop, colliding with his chest.

He ringed his arms reflexively around the tall, female body.

He kept holding on because the blue eyes pleading with his froze him in place. The scent of her shampoo mixed with the aroma of coffee. Lazy Sunday mornings with Stella would smell like that. Lying in bed, letting their beverages get cold while they kept each other warm.

Not if she's on the other side of the country.

But it was more than geography. She didn't want *him.* She'd made that clear.

He stepped back, feeling the gazes of every person in the shop boring into him.

Her face fell. "We need to talk."

"We already did," he said through gritted teeth.

"Ryan? Is there anything we can do?" Gran asked, watching him with interest.

"Absolutely nothing. You can do absolutely nothing," he replied.

Georgie tipped her hat and took his grandmother by the elbow. "You got it."

The two women left.

"Shouldn't you be gone by now?" he murmured to Stella.

Her mouth parted, and a murmur of regret escaped.

Do not think of kissing those lips. It's not enough.

"You told me to ask you for help with my case if I needed it," she said, voice edging on a plea. "But I think I need your help with something else."

The paper bag in his hand crinkled as he gripped it. "Go back to New York, Stella. Figure out your life there, and if you're willing to believe in what we could be, then we can talk." He turned and headed for the back door instead. He skirted the counter and glass case and reached for the door handle.

"Wait!" she called. "Is you coming to New York still a possibility?"

The usual coffee-shop buzz silenced. The clinking of cups and cutlery being put down rang out. A few people started whispering. Stella tried to tune it out, focus only on Ryan, but it was hard to miss.

"…leaving…?"

"…election…"

"Wasn't she mentioned on CNN last night?"

Ryan froze, back to her, shoulders rigid.

Oh, crap. She had not meant to announce him coming to Manhattan in front of the Peak Beans' clientele. She'd intended to make it known *she* was ready to make changes, not to ask him to do it.

"That's not what I meant!" she projected, using her "calm the chatty boardroom" voice. Making the entire town panic would not win her his heart, nor would living in New York make him happy. It had been an excellent place for her to succeed, and she'd always love it for the bustle and diversity and rich culture, but her family was right—that wasn't what she needed right now. She couldn't grow her roots without people she loved around her, and while for some the city could be a wonderful place to find community, that wasn't what it had been for her. She'd used the busyness and noise to numb herself. It was time to face her past, and look forward to the present. And she wanted to do that with Ryan at her side.

"I'm not going to steal your sheriff." She spoke loud enough for the curious crowd to hear. "But I do love him—"

The desperation crossing Ryan's handsome face stopped her, a silent plea for her to stop.

He doesn't want this... But she had a flight to catch in two hours—she was cutting it way too close to turn away now. Hurrying through the café, she willed him not to retreat farther.

"Please hear me out." She could detect the choppiness of her words, but her breath was coming quick and her pulse was racing, and somehow this felt like the most important thing she'd do in her life—

Because it is.

Ryan glanced over her head, scanning the room and frowning. Taking her by the elbow, he tugged her down the hall to the washrooms and staff area.

He leaned a shoulder against the wall, arms crossed. "Kinda public, Stella."

"I'm sorry. I didn't know what else to do. I have all of five minutes until I have to leave, and I know this sheriff who's a stickler for speed limits—"

His eyebrows lifted. "With reason."

"Sure. But this sheriff… I love him. And I had to tell him."

Mouth gaping, he let out a hissing breath. "I—I don't know what to say."

"You don't need to say anything. I'm the one who has ground to make up."

He scrubbed a hand down his face before crossing his arms again. "I thought you needed to get back to New York and solve your crisis before you make any decisions."

She shook her head, wringing her hands to stop from reaching for him. "I figured it out without going."

"Didn't take long."

"It's taken eighteen years, Ryan. That's plenty long enough. And it's been a long time coming. It just took getting out of the shell I've built for myself to realize that I wasn't content with my life. Success isn't enough anymore. The idea of spending the next few years fighting my way into people's good graces again—that sounds so freaking lonely. And…I'm tired of being lonely."

He wore his caution like a smoke screen, a barrier between them. His mouth pinched, the look on his face grim and uncertain. "People behave badly sometimes. I've been that person. But if you're willing to slough off me baring my soul in public, it's hard for me to believe that you love me."

Her heart wobbled. "I know. You'll just have to trust me, I guess."

He barked out a dry laugh. "Pretty sure we agreed that *you* trusting *me* was the problem."

She held back a curse. She was losing him, wasn't doing enough… "I was hoping… In a couple of weeks, after my meeting tomorrow and once I do a whole lot of wrangling with my lawyers and the investigation team, would you come help pack my apartment?"

His impassive reaction made her eyes sting.

"Stupid idea," she said, cursing. "As if you can get holidays at short notice. Forget I asked."

He bent toward her and hooked her wrist, pulling her within inches of his body. The thin line of his lips contradicted his leaning posture and the loose, relaxed hold on her hand. Her left hand. He traced the base of her ring finger with the pad of his thumb, as if imagining the wedding ring she'd once hoped he'd place there.

Her pulse skipped, and she waited. Pressure built in her stomach. Seconds ticked, and the deep blue scrutiny became unbearable.

"What?" The word burst out. "Please. Tell me something. I have—" she pulled her phone from the pocket of her coat and checked the time "—two minutes. And I need way more time than that with you. A lifetime, really."

"A lifetime's not going to fit into a hundred and twenty seconds, doll," he said quietly, grip tightening on her hand. "Hell, you telling me how you figure you'll be able to live here and be happy will take a whole lot longer than that, too."

"I know. And I want to give you more. I do. I want to give you all of me. But I can't reschedule that meeting tomorrow. Not if I'm going to give myself the best chance to walk away with compensation—"

"Walk away? And here that's what I thought you were doing to me." He looped his arm around her waist and tucked her in the nook between his body and the wall. Leaning as he was, they were face-to-face. She took the chance and kissed him softly.

His eyes fluttered closed, and his breath caught audibly. Cupping her cheek with a tender hand, he deepened the kiss.

Spending their last two minutes doing this might not convince him that she was sincere, but at least it felt—

No. This wasn't why she'd tracked him down. She pulled her mouth away. Her body complained at the distance, but she refocused.

"I'm not walking away from you for long. I'll be *joining* you. And Lach and Maggie, too. Joining their business, growing it—I want to start a life here. With you. But I can't think of some grand gesture to prove it."

He chuckled, burying his face in the crook of her neck. His breath brushed her skin, sending shivers down her limbs. "Fine by me. You shouting that you love me to the entire coffee shop was beyond public enough for my liking."

She winced. "You were escaping, and I couldn't let—"

"It's okay, Stella. People are interested because they care. And having the fact you love me be public knowledge? I like that. More than you know. But proving love? That'll happen over time, don't you think? Slowly?"

"Bit hard to be slow when I'm going to need to move across the country."

He smiled. "And you want me to help you with that?"

She nodded. "If you can."

"If taking a rotation off for family leave means getting you home faster, I'll make it happen."

Family. The word bloomed in her chest, her emotions around it complicated and nuanced, as always. But she was getting used to the positive connotations. Focusing not on the pain and isolation she'd attached to it in the past, but on what it meant now, and what it would mean in the future. Connection. Security.

Joy.

She kissed him again. "I'd have to be your family for you to get leave without lying."

"Are you planning to wake up in my bed every morning?"

His stern tone made her laugh. "Yes, Sheriff."

"With no plans to stop?"

She stroked his face, his short beard soft under her hand. The sensation grounded her in the reality of this—it was really happening. And she couldn't be more at peace about it. "You're stuck with me," she teased.

His expression stayed serious. "And a couple of years from now, could we look to turning the spare room into a nursery?"

Warmth infused her at the thought of welcoming a child or two with Ryan. "I'd love to."

"Me, too." He bent his head and kissed her cheek. His whisper was a caress, a promise. "That sounds like family to me."

Epilogue

Six months later

The afternoon of the training school's grand opening, Stella raced around the clinic building into the
yard. She'd been in charge of bringing dessert, and
had gotten held up at the Main Street Bakery—
anyone who wasn't here was there, lining up for
the epically popular wedding cupcakes Ryan's aunt
Nancy had been churning out for weeks to com-
memorate Gertie and Gramps having tied the knot
in Las Vegas almost a month ago. Wedding bells
were definitely in the air. Ryan had been dropping
hints like nobody's business. But with Maggie and
Asher planning to say their vows in the fall, and her

grandfather still wearing his new-groom glow, Stella hadn't felt the need to hurry.

Until this morning, anyway.

Her other reason for being late to the party—she was late in the way that mattered most.

She'd been so shocked, staring at the pregnancy test on the bathroom counter, she'd been tardy leaving to get the desserts in the first place. She and Ryan had figured it might take them a while to get pregnant, so they'd gotten a little fast and loose with protection. She should have at least anticipated that things could happen faster than they'd expected... But maybe the test was wrong. Her period had been due yesterday—what was one day?

It wasn't wrong. Those lines were nice and clear.

Knowing Ryan, he'd want to keep this private. Hell, she did, too. It was way too early to announce anything. She wasn't about to tell half the town that she was expecting, so she wouldn't be telling him during the party. But how would she be able to keep it to herself when her heart was bursting? She'd have to hide it, somehow.

Careful not to jar the extralarge box of dog-shaped cookies and puppy-themed cake pops, Stella halted at the edge of the rectangular lawn and groaned. Her stilettos were the worst choice for wearing on the grass. But she'd started the day with a meeting at the bank about the newly formed Gallatin Paws Foundation before heading home, boxed pregnancy test in hand. And had been so discombobulated after seeing those blue lines that she hadn't changed out of her skirt and heels as planned.

Her sister sidled over and held out a pair of her work clogs. "Trade you. I heard you clicking all the way from the parking lot. Figured you could use these."

Stella handed over the box and took the shoes in return. She toed out of her heels and slid into Maggie's flat-soled offering. "Better. Thanks."

The July sky was overcast, but Maggie was smiling bright enough to make up for the lack of sunlight. So was their brother, for that matter, as he stood across the lawn with his family.

Her family. Her siblings and their significant others and kids, their grandparents and the more distant connections, too. Asher's brother, Caleb, and his partner, Garnet, who was pregnant with their first child and just starting to show. Marisol's brother, Zach, and his wife, Cadie, chasing after their little one and, rumor had it, considering having another. And the whole Halloran crew was here, except for Georgie and her husband, who were off on a three-month adventure in Europe. The lawn was crawling with people who were connected through blood and marriage. So much love.

She'd been foolish, thinking that she didn't need it or want it. And was lucky as anything to have been absorbed into the fold. And to be adding to it… Unbelievable.

She gave her sister a side hug. "Good to know we'll all fit back here for your wedding."

Maggie tipped her head onto Stella's shoulder. "Good to know *you'll* be standing next to me when it happens." She cleared her throat. "I'd better get these cookies over to the food table before the hungry masses revolt."

Stella motioned her sister forward, stood on her toes and scanned the crowd, frowning. The man most integral to her life was nowhere to be seen. She deposited her shoes and purse under a folding chair and peered around bodies, looking for the black, short-sleeved uniform shirt Ryan had been wearing when he'd left the house this morning. Unless he'd changed—

A pair of strong arms linked around her waist, pulling her against a hard chest and the distinct lack of a weapons belt.

"Hey, Bella," Ryan murmured in her ear.

She reached back and ran her hands down his sides from waist to hips, finding a T-shirt and some lightweight shorts. "You went home."

Wait, had he seen the test in the bathroom garbage? Her pulse raced.

"You didn't." He clucked his disapproval. "And here I was hoping to take those shoes off you myself."

"I can put them back on later."

"Do that." He dropped a lazy kiss to her temple.

"Big turnout. I imagine my aunts and their broods will turn up when the bakery closes."

"Mmm-hmm," she hummed, afraid if she opened her mouth, she'd blurt out that more of his family was here than he realized. Good grief. Once she'd committed sharing everything that mattered with this man, she'd gotten really terrible at hiding things. And he was so attuned to facial expressions, hers especially. As soon as he got a good look at her eyes, he'd know something was up.

Attempting to school the blend of nerves and excitement pulling at her mouth, she relaxed into him. "I was saying to Maggie that it's good to see the yard full of people. Gives them an idea of what to expect for the wedding."

"Yeah." He pointed over to the fenced-off field beyond the newly-built barn. "That'd be a nice place for a ceremony."

The statement was weighted.

And if she all of a sudden showed her eagerness to get a ring on her finger, he'd ask her what made her want to speed up—

She shrugged, feigning being noncommittal. She motioned toward Laura, who held Lachlan's finger on one side and Marisol's on the other, and was taking a few tentative steps, much to her parents' delight. "Laura is pretty much the cutest."

"Oh, I don't know. I'm betting ours would be cuter."

She froze. Tilting her head, she peered at him

from the corner of her eye. His smile was relaxed. Not ecstatic, like it would be had he guessed, or seen that test. Breathing a sigh of relief, she said as blandly as possible, "That'll be a ways off, though."

"I guess." He sighed and ran a palm along her belly.

Her knees went mushy and she held in a squeak of contentment.

"I thought we were starting to think about kids," he said, tone low with disappointment.

"Start thinking? No."

He tightened his hold on her and exhaled. "Well, you let me know, sweetheart."

Ouch. Time for a rethink. She couldn't keep him in the dark if he was going to be so sad… Turning in his embrace, she cupped his face. "Come for a walk with me."

He shook his head. "Food first, okay? I'm starving." He nudged her toward the table weighed down with trays of ribs and salads.

Stopping him with a hand to his chest, she fixed him with a meaningful look and said, "We should really find a quiet corner."

Crossing his arms, he frowned. "Stella…"

A major rethink, then. "If I tell you something, promise you won't react?"

His brow crinkled. "I spend my whole workday facing the unbelievable and manage to keep a stone face. What's wrong?"

"Nothing." She put her hands on his shoulders

and went up on her toes, as close to his ear as she could get. "We're beyond 'starting to think' about having kids. I'm ready. Which is a damn good thing, because by next spring, you're going to be a daddy."

He stumbled back a step and his jaw dropped. "Did you say *daddy*?"

Heads turned in their direction.

"Shh!" She motioned for him to keep his voice down. "I said not to react. It's super early. Like, 'happened at the cabin on the Fourth when we were lazy about condoms' early. What happened to stone-faced Ryan?"

His mouth gaped and he cupped her cheeks with both hands, stroking with his thumbs. "Fatherhood, doll. And not expecting it this soon."

Her stomach twinged and she wrung her hands. "Will it be okay?"

"Stella." Covering her hands with a big palm, he squeezed. Then he pressed his lips to her forehead, a long, tender touch punctuated by a deep breath through his nose. "You even need to ask?"

"Well, yeah. I figured you'd at least smile."

He finally did. A sheepish, overwhelmed lip tilt that he covered with shaking fingers. She felt it through her whole body, a rush of the magnitude of what they were going to take on.

He glanced at her stomach. "You're— Wow. Just wow."

"I know. I took the test right after I finished at the

bank, and I almost peed myself with surprise, except I'd just gone, and…"

He chuckled. "We can spend the rest of our lives surprising each other, okay?"

Wrapping her arms around his waist, she let herself be absorbed by his warmth and the smell of fresh T-shirt and Ryan. "And loving each other. Every day."

"Sounds like everything I ever wanted."

* * * * *

Don't miss the previous titles in Laurel Greer's Sutter Creek, Montana miniseries:

From Exes to Expecting
A Father for Her Child
Holiday by Candlelight
Their Nine-Month Surprise
In Service of Love

Available now from Harlequin Special Edition!

"And your secluded mountainside home with the
fancy electronics is part of that safety net? And your
hellhound?"

Jillie chuckled, looking up to where Sophie was
glaring down at Matt from the deck. "Don't insult my
dog. She's more for companionship than protection.
Although her appearance doesn't hurt." She shuddered
and pulled her jacket tighter.

God, he'd kept her standing out here in the cold and
dark while he grilled her with questions. She'd already
hinted that it was time for him to go. He scrubbed his
hands down his face.

"I'm sorry, Jillie. You must be freezing. Go on up.
Once I know you're inside, I'll take off."

"And you were on your way to dinner. You must
be starving." She hesitated for just a moment. In that
moment, he *really* wanted her to invite him up to join

her for dinner, but that didn't happen. Instead, she flashed him a quick smile before turning to go. "Thanks again, Matt."

Let her walk away. Way too complicated. Just let her walk away.

She was all the way up to the deck when he heard his own voice calling out to her.

"The old ski lift is working well, but I need to give it a few test runs, just to get acquainted with the thing. If you want a ride up to that craggy summit you like so much, I'll be heading up there Sunday afternoon. It'll just be us. No workers. No spectators."

Her head started to move back and forth, then stopped. She looked down at him in silence, then gave a loud sigh. "Maybe. I'll let you know. I've…I've got to go in."

He watched her and Sophie go through the door. She turned and locked it, then gave him a stuttering wave. For someone obsessed with privacy, it was interesting that this entire wall, right up to the peak of the A-frame roof, was glass. He lifted his hand, then headed to his car. He wasn't sure what surprised him more. That he'd asked Jillie to ride to the top of the mountain with him, or that she'd said maybe. As he turned the ignition, he realized he was smiling.

Don't miss
Her Mountainside Haven *by Jo McNally,*
available February 2021 wherever
Harlequin Special Edition books and ebooks are sold.

Harlequin.com

Get 4 **FREE REWARDS!**

We'll send you 2 FREE Books
plus 2 FREE Mystery Gifts.

Harlequin Special Edition
books relate to finding
comfort and strength in
the support of loved ones
and enjoying the journey
no matter what life throws
your way.

FREE
Value Over
$20

YES! Please send me 2 FREE Harlequin Special Edition novels and my 2 FREE gifts (gifts are worth about $10 retail). After receiving them, if I don't wish to receive any more books, I can return the shipping statement marked "cancel." If I don't cancel, I will receive 6 brand-new novels every month and be billed just $4.99 per book in the U.S. or $5.74 per book in Canada. That's a savings of at least 12% off the cover price! It's quite a bargain! Shipping and handling is just 50¢ per book in the U.S. and $1.25 per book in Canada.* I understand that accepting the 2 free books and gifts places me under no obligation to buy anything. I can always return a shipment and cancel at any time. The free books and gifts are mine to keep no matter what I decide.

235/335 HDN GNMP

Name (please print)

Address _____ Apt. #

City _____ State/Province _____ Zip/Postal Code

Email: Please check this box ☐ if you would like to receive newsletters and promotional emails from Harlequin Enterprises ULC and its affiliates. You can unsubscribe anytime.

Mail to the **Reader Service:**
IN U.S.A.: P.O. Box 1341, Buffalo, NY 14240-8531
IN CANADA: P.O. Box 603, Fort Erie, Ontario L2A 5X3

Want to try 2 free books from another series! Call 1-800-873-8635 or visit www.ReaderService.com.

*Terms and prices subject to change without notice. Prices do not include sales taxes, which will be charged (if applicable) based on your state or country of residence. Canadian residents will be charged applicable taxes. Offer not valid in Quebec. This offer is limited to one order per household. Books received may not be as shown. Not valid for current subscribers to Harlequin Special Edition books. All orders subject to approval. Credit or debit balances in a customer's account(s) may be offset by any other outstanding balance owed by or to the customer. Please allow 4 to 6 weeks for delivery. Offer available while quantities last.

Your Privacy—Your information is being collected by Harlequin Enterprises ULC, operating as Reader Service. For a complete summary of the information we collect, how we use this information and to whom it is disclosed, please visit our privacy notice located at corporate.harlequin.com/privacy-notice. From time to time we may also exchange your personal information with reputable third parties. If you wish to opt out of this sharing of your personal information, please visit readerservice.com/consumerchoice or call 1-800-873-8635. **Notice to California Residents**—Under California law, you have specific rights to control and access your data. For more information on these rights and how to exercise them, visit corporate.harlequin.com/california-privacy.

HSE20R2

IF YOU ENJOYED THIS BOOK
WE THINK YOU WILL ALSO LOVE

LOVE INSPIRED
INSPIRATIONAL ROMANCE

Uplifting stories of faith, forgiveness and hope.

Fall in love with stories where faith helps
guide you through life's challenges, and discover
the promise of a new beginning.

6 NEW BOOKS AVAILABLE EVERY MONTH!

In high school, Finn had dated a girl for about six months. Once, when they'd been watching a movie, she'd fallen asleep tucked against his arm. His arm had also fallen asleep. It had been a painfully good place to be, and he hadn't moved even though he'd suffered through the end of that movie.

This time it was three little monkeys who'd taken over his personal space, and once again he was incredibly uncomfortable and strangely content at the same time.

Reese, the most cautious of the three, had snuggled against his side. She'd fallen asleep first, and her little features were so peaceful that his grinch's heart had grown three sizes.

Lola had been trying to make it to the end of the movie, fighting back heavy eyelids and extended yawns, but eventually she'd conked out.

Sage was the only one still standing, though her fidgeting from the back of the couch had lessened considerably.

Ivy returned from the bunkhouse. She'd taken a couple of trips over with laundry as the movie finished and now returned the basket to his laundry room. She walked into the living room as the movie credits rolled and turned off the TV.

"Guess I let them stay up too late." She moved to sit on the coffee table, facing him. "I'll carry Lola and Reese back. Sage, you can walk, can't you, love?"

Sage's weighted lids said the battle to stay awake had been hard fought. "I hold you, too, Mommy."

Cute. Finn wouldn't mind following that rabbit trail. Wouldn't mind making the same request of Ivy. Despite his determination not to let her burrow under his skin, tonight she'd done exactly that. He'd found himself attending the school of Ivy when she was otherwise distracted. Did she know that she made the tiniest sound popping her lips when she was lost in thought? Or that she tilted her head to the right and only the right when she was listening— and studied the speaker with so much interest that it made them feel like the most important human on the planet?

Stay on track, Brightwood. This isn't your circus. Finn had already bought a ticket to a circus back in North Dakota, and things hadn't ended well. No need to attend that show again. Especially when the price of admission had cost him so much.

"I'll help carry. I can take two if you take one."

"Thank you. That would be really great. I'd prefer to move them into their beds and keep them asleep if at all possible. If Reese gets woken up, she'll start crying, and I'm not sure I have the bandwidth for that tonight."

Ivy gathered the girls' movie and sweatshirts, then slipped Sage from the back of the couch.

Finn scooped up Reese and caught Lola with his other arm. He stood and held still, waiting for complaints. Lola fidgeted and then settled back to peaceful. Reese was so far gone that she didn't even flinch.

These girls. His dry, brittle heart cracked and healed all at the same time. They were good for the soul.

Don't miss
Choosing His Family *by Jill Lynn,*
available February 2021 wherever
Love Inspired books and ebooks are sold.

LoveInspired.com

LIEXP0121